THE RAVENS OF FALKENAU
and Other Stories

JO GRAHAM

Crossroad Press

I went over and blew out the candle at the window sill. In the sudden burst of light as the flame was extinguished I saw the reflection of the fourth man. I would have thought it was one of our troopers, except for the shadow of folded wings behind him, cast high on the wall.

I turned.

He wore bloodstained velvet and a breastplate of good Spanish steel, light brown hair framing a tired young face, lined with care and weal. A blackened swept hilt rapier was at his side. His voice was very cool. "You should have a care, summoning your betters. It's not polite."

"My Lord," I said, "I do not believe in you."

Something moved in his eyes, some expression of regret. "Do you not?" he said, "Son of my heart? Can you have forgotten yourself so much?"

"I have forgotten nothing," I said, and a great anger rose in me, the battle blindness I sometimes feel, pure and hot as fire. "Where were you when my stepfather beat me bloody again and again? Where were you when his fists blinded my mother and broke her jaw? When I killed him as he stood, when I was fifteen, and still she wept and said that she should turn me over to the Graf's men for a murderer so that I should hang for killing him? Where were you when I fled from that place with nothing but my shirt and a bloody knife to make my way in this world?" I turned away from him. "I would that you were more than drunken imaginings so that I might put this blade through you."

CONTENTS

"Don't the great tales ever end?"
"No, they never end as tales, but the people in them come and go when their part's ended."

—J.R.R. Tolkien

INTRODUCTION

The world is a numinous place, for those who have eyes to
see it.

Welcome to the Numinous World, where gods and angels
intervene in the lives of mortals, and a band of eternal companions
unite and reunite over the centuries, striving to make the world
a better place despite wars and dark ages, hatred and cruelty.
Here are stories from the very beginning of our history, when
the Lady of Cats entered the life of a young woman and changed
her forever, long ago when farmers first scraped a living from
the soil. Here too are stories of the ancient world—of Dion, the
peerless scientist of Alexandria, of Lucia, a Roman waif, of a
Persian princess and her Jewish sister in law, of Lydias of Miletus
who is once and always Ptolemy's man, and of a Nubian girl
who begins a long journey toward a strange destiny. There are
stories of the Dark Ages, of a last Roman outpost on the shores of
Britain and of an Arab warrior who at last comes home to a white
city on the sea, of a Scottish witch who serves the Storm Queen
and fears no other magic, and a Knight Templar enslaved by the
beauty of the world. Others follow—a messenger boy dragged
into the Great Story and a desperate ride dogged by the Wild
Hunt, and a mercenary captain of the Thirty Years War who
finds his destiny in a remote corner of the Bohemian mountains.
Here too are more modern tales of the Age of Revolution, when
Dion, Emrys, Sigismund and Charmian reunite in Napoleonic
Paris, and at last we roll into the twentieth century with a young

American girl with extraordinary oracular powers. Of course there is also Michael, Mik-el, Mikhael, who watches over his charges as best he may, though the world may change around them.

These are tiny windows into a miraculous world, glimpses through a glass and darkly of all that might be—for those with eyes to see. I hope you enjoy the journey!

THE RAVENS OF FALKENAU

1614-1634 AD

This is one of the oldest stories in the Numinous World, in the sense of having been begun first. I started it in 1995 when I was working at an exceedingly boring temp job. I couldn't put anything personal on their computers, so it was written in longhand on a yellow legal pad and then finished more than fifteen years later. In many ways Georg is the darkest version of our main character. It has been a long time since Black Ships, *and the road has not been kind.*

I was seventeen when I first came to Falkenau, in the Year of Our Lord 1614, the second year of the old Emperor Matthias, the last king before the wars of religion began. I was young and unemployed, another hopeful boy pursuing the trade of arms unsuccessfully, hoping to make enough in bounty and plunder to live well before I died.

Falkenau was a medieval fortress high in the mountains, situated on a crag swept about on three sides by a river now frozen and pale with a dusting of snow that rested on the ice. There was a village as well, not large, with the usual steep, muddy streets with goats everywhere, and the Church of the Virgin beneath its pitched roof and mushroom dome.

In the summer I'm sure it was all very pretty, but in January it was nothing but cold. We would not have come to Falkenau at all, my companions and I, if the Prince of Anhalt-Bernberg hadn't discharged us in September without even a bonus, and by January money was running out. Rumor had it in the coffeehouses of Prague, which were much warmer and more pleasant, but much less profitable, that the old lord of Falkenau was looking for armsmen, but by the time we got there he had already finished hiring everyone he wanted.

I was ready to leave again, but Marik advised against it.

"Just sit still, boy," he said, putting one hand on my shoulder as we negotiated our way back down the steep road that led to the castle. "Have a little patience."

"I'd have more patience if I had more kroner," I replied. The sack at my belt was nearly empty.

"Some of those bastards he hired won't work out," Marik said. "Just watch and see. In a week he'll have to turn out four or five for drunkenness and then we'll move into their positions. It's a matter of being in the right place at the right time."

I shrugged. "I'm never in the right place at the right time." Beneath me the frozen trickle of water looked blue against the stones, and the valley was encased in snow. I'd sold my horse seven weeks before.

Marik seized my sleeve and pulled me back from the edge, from the leap I hadn't really thought about making. "You will be, son. You've good eyes, good health, a good mind and a way with horses. If you don't do something stupid you'll see thirty."

I shrugged. "And so? What then? I wind up too old to fight with a mess of scars to prove it, broke as I am now, with what to show for it?"

Marik gave me a hard look beneath his bushy brows. "So what did you leave home for?"

"Nothing to leave," I said. I would not talk about that. Ever. "I went to win my fortune," I said.

On that day in the spring two years before, Captain Sylvester

Von Boren was hiring, set up at the best inn in town, a mug of hot wine at his elbow, the lace on his cuffs dripping down over his hands. I joined in the line of ragged plowboys, university students, and grizzled middle aged men snaking its way toward the long table where the celebrated captain sat, resplendent in buff and scarlet, captured Mongol gold spread out before him for an inducement, with a young priest at his elbow to write in a fair hand the names of those joining the company, their skills, pay and terms. As each man stepped up the captain had a word with him, sometimes for a few minutes, sometimes only for a second or two. The grizzled veterans he sent to his right, to the priest, with no hesitation. The others fared less well. Most shuffled away, disgruntled. Only a few took the priest's quill in hand to make their mark next to their name and sign their life away for ten gold kroner, a knife and pick, and a full suit of clothes.

I noted, hopefully, that most only make an *X*. I could at least write my name. So could the university students. The plowboys never got a chance. I was acutely aware of the ten pounds of aged metal strapped to my side, a heavy iron sword I bought off old man Gottfried when I left home, who had used it in the last century. It was a pretension to gentility.

At last it was my turn. The captain's blue eyes flicked up and down me once, taking in my faded brown coat, my scraggling attempt at a dashing moustache. "Your name, boy?"

"Georg," I managed, trying to make my voice come out deep and manly instead of the pleasant tenor I'm cursed with.

The captain sighed wearily. "Georg what?"

I thought of the cobbler's house I had grown up in, the refuse in the street, the hens picking in the gutter. High above the town I was born in, Marianburg Fortress reared its head, with strong walls and the little chapel that was older than the Son of

God, Corinthian columns about the statue of the Virgin.

"Von Marianburg," I said, straightening my back. "Georg Von Marianburg."

There was a glimmer of interest in the captain's eyes. "What can you do, Georg Von Marianburg?"

I swallowed. "I have a strong back and I'm good with horses. I can fight and I have shot a musket and I can write my name as well."

"Can you use that chunk of metal you're wearing?" rumbled a blond, bearded man behind the captain, the company's Second, a Dane named Shorty who wasn't.

I swallowed again. "Yes," I said.

The Dane snorted. "Hardly worth the trouble, Captain."

Von Boren shrugged and reached for his mug.

"Wait!" I said, desperate not to be turned away as so many had been. "I'll fight for my place."

The captain looked up, startled.

"To first blood," I amended. "Any man you choose. It's my risk. But if I put up a good showing you'll make a place for me."

The Dane chuckled.

"Done," the captain said, rising to his feet. "It was near time to take a break from so much sitting. This will at least prove entertaining. Shorty, will you take him?"

The Second gestured to his beautiful blue velvet doublet. "Me? I've small desire to spoil my new clothes with blood and sweat, even if it be another's. Let Lukan do it." He gestured to a smaller man of indeterminate nationality who grinned at me with two black teeth between gray lips.

"Out in the yard, then," the captain said, walking around the table, his suede boots making no sound on the floor.

We went out into the stone courtyard of the inn, a bit of the crowd following us, hooting derisively. I pretended I could not hear them, and truthfully I really could not, seized as I was by a curious sense of unreality. I could get killed here, I thought. That would be a useless end to a useless existence. There was no one in the world besides myself it would matter to. I could not believe that it would matter to God.

Lukan tossed his coat to a friend of his who stood by. I had no friend, so I kept mine on.

With a grin, Lukan unsheathed his sword. It was lighter than mine, but longer, Italian in design, with a swept hilt. I hoped he wouldn't kill me.

He raised the blade in ironic salute, then stepped forward, the blade whistling past my eyes as I stepped back.

Then I went absolutely cold.

I swung at him with all my strength, connecting with his blade with a shock and a ringing sound like bells, flailing at him like a battering ram. His blade was faster, his responses much cleaner. I did not see or think, only reacted, as though my entire self were concentrated in my hand instead of my head, as though this was a dance I had known all my life.

I could not hear the crowd. All I could hear was the whistle of his blade, and the sound as it connected with the pommel of my sword, wrenching it from my hand and sending it clattering across the cobblestones.

"Hold!" the captain said.

I stopped, my breath loud in my ears.

Lukan lowered his blade. "This boy flails around like he's threshing wheat," he said.

"Like he's got a damned broadsword," the Dane muttered.

I felt something moving against my chin and brushed it away, surprised to see my hand come away bloody.

Lukan stepped across the distance between us. "I got you with the tip on my first attack. You didn't even feel it." He handed me a linen square from his pocket. It took me a moment to realize it was a handkerchief.

"Where do you come from, boy?" the Dane asked.

I dabbed cautiously at the cut on my chin, which still didn't hurt. "My father was in the service of the King of Saxony," I replied. "He was killed fighting the Tartars in Wallachia." Which was all entirely untrue, as my father was a cobbler and died when I was six.

The Dane raised skeptical eyebrows. "And then? You fell on hard times?"

I looked down at my shabby peasant clothes and tried to stand straighter, as befitted a young nobleman bereft of everything in the world but his name and his pride. "Very hard, sir."

The Captain frowned. "Have you no family to object to your taking a position as a common soldier?"

"None, sir." I did not have to lie about that. "My mother died recently. I have no other family."

Lukan looked at the Dane and shrugged. Shorty raised an eyebrow. I held my breath.

"Oh very well," the captain said. "Father, read him in and pay him. Shorty, you'll have to do something about that sword. He thinks it's the Goddamned Crusades. Read him in and pay him off." The captain turned and strode away.

That is how I joined Von Boren's company, when I was just short of sixteen. I know this, because it was March then, and I was born under the sign of the Bull in the fullness of spring in the year 1596.

That summer we fought for one of the Lusatian princes in his quarrel with his brother-in-law. I learned to fire a musket propped on a tripod, to disassemble it, clean it, and coat it with warm oil, to keep powder dry and match alight. I could hit the target better than some, but also worse than some, not that anyone hit often with those hideously inaccurate guns.

That fall we were paid in full, quartered decently, and in the spring we sacked Cottbus for the Margrave of Brandenburg. I won a horse there, which I could ride, and also killed two civilians, which made me sick, though not too sick to take their gold.

I was seventeen then, a man grown. I would never be large, as few of us Bavarians are, but my beard came in dark and glossy and covered the scar on my chin. I killed a Swede in a tavern fight in Prague after the captain was killed and the Duke turned us off, so it was all for the best that Marik and I, and three other men of the company, went up to Falkenau.

That night we made merry in the best inn in town, while the townsmen watched us suspiciously, as out of work mercenaries don't have a reputation for keeping the peace. Outside the snow was falling soundlessly. All you could see of the fortress were some distant lights on the crag.

Marik, of course, had found someone he knew who was in the Old Lord's employ and was offering him good wine by the fire and pumping him for information.

I sat staring idly out the front window, warming my hands around my cup and wondering why the barmaid was both unfriendly and a hag, listening to Marik and the guardsman with half an ear.

"Old days!" the guardsman said, lifting his cup, Marik following suit.

"Old days! Things aren't like they used to be!"

"No, indeed." The guardsman drank. "Everything goes from bad to worse."

"Does it?" Marik said. "I thought you had it good, with a nice permanent post at arms for a lord with money to spend."

"Not so much money as that," the guardsman said, and drank again. "And not much mood for spending it."

"Oh?" Marik asked, refilling his cup. "Why's that?"

"He lost his lady wife scarce a sevenday ago. Childbed. Poor woman threw five sons in a row, and not one of them saw his first birthday. Now she's had a girl and died of it. The Lord's like to lose his mind."

"A hard thing. Hard thing," Marik sympathized.

I took another long drink, waiting for the familiar feeling of the world tilting in good red wine.

The garrulous guardsman continued. "Most likely this babe will die, same as the others. Then he'll have no heir."

"No heir's the same as a girl child," Marik said.

"It's said she's a sickly thing," the guardsman said sadly.

The swirling snow made shapes out of wind. There were lights in the high towers of the fortress.

Somewhere up there the Lord in his comfortable rooms lost his wife in winter, and the last of his line lay near death, a sickly babe in a cradle lined in velvet.

"Death," I said softly, and toasted the distant lights in the snow.

It was nineteen years before I came back to Falkenau.

I took service with the King of Poland to hold back the Tartars, and spent four years fighting up and down Silesia for his gold and a long scar on my sword arm. I learned to ride like a Pole, which is to say as if I'd been born on horseback, and decided to live no other way unless necessity forced me. I loved a girl in Warsaw who played me false, and I went away to war again.

In Prague the young King of Bohemia, Frederick, and his Protestant English bride took on the might of the Holy Roman Emperor, and angry townsmen threw the Pope's men out the windows of the hall. I served Frederick and his bride, Elizabeth, the Winter Queen, with a joy I saw no reason for. It was right to me, and fair that her name was Elizabeth, and she was beleaguered and alone, but she was no tactician. In the end they fled, and Marik died in their last battle, covering the Queen's retreat, and I had had enough of queens.

I won a blackened Italian rapier off a corpse in Brandenburg, and a fine Andalusian horse from the Palatine cavalry. I loved a girl in Ulm, left her with child, returned and found her dead, and I had had enough of women.

The Protestant princes allied against the Holy Roman Emperor, and the King of Sweden joined them. I had a company now, all cavalry, in buff and black. I wore French lace at my cuffs now, and sat in inns deciding who should live and who should die.

We joined the Catholic army when Gustavus Adolphus, the King of Sweden, landed. I could care less whose God won.

More interesting to me were the stars and their endless patterns, wherein a wise man could read the future and a foolish man see hopes. Alchemy interested me too, and history. My hand became fair from reading and writing dispatches, and at night when I could not sleep I read whatever came to hand— war and passion, descriptions of new lands across the seas for the winning, legends and bloody histories of things that happened long ago.

Sometimes, in the darkness, they took on life to me and it seemed that I had lived there and been a part of those tales. Somewhere in the west I had died in Templar's mail at a contested river ford, or hidden restless in high Scottish hills, a bowman fighting for an exiled king. It seemed I had knelt breathless before a red-haired princess, or in woman's body borne a child in white Alexandria under a scorching sun, stood veiled on a galley sailing through crystal seas. But these were fancies, and did little more than beguile my dreams when all I could think of were battles.

In the early spring just before my twenty-ninth birthday I was called into Prague. The Emperor had given command of all his forces to a new Generalissimo, Wallenstein, a mercenary who had begun fighting the Turks. He was the greatest soldier of the age.

He was in his fifties then, lean and supple with the bitter strength of a man who has spent his youth at war and his age in courts. He had black eyes and a firm handshake.

"Please sit down, Captain Von Marianburg," he said, gesturing to one of the two great carved chairs before the fire.

I sat down opposite him then, taking care not to singe the Belgian lace at my boot tops on the fender.

He wore a huge ruby on his hand that exactly matched the crimson sash of the Imperial army. "You come to me recommended," he said, "by Count Trcka, a very trustworthy soldier."

I did not answer, only waited for him to continue.

He watched me sharply. "You fought in Poland, I understand."

"I did," I replied.

"Against the infidel," he said.

"Yes," I agreed. "But I do not care much for all that. One

God is as good as another."

Wallenstein laughed. "You are not a patriot, then."

"I am a mercenary," I said. "I fight for gold. If you have heard that I will not commit my men to a hopeless fight, it is a matter of economics, that's all. I would be foolish to squander my livelihood."

Wallenstein smiled thinly. "Yet you claim a nobleman's name and honor."

"As do you," I replied.

He laughed then and ordered the servant to pour us French brandy. Then he dismissed the man. "The Emperor," he said abruptly, "is a fool. So is the Pope. I could care less who sits on either throne. But I am Bohemian, and I have grown tired of Bohemia spoiled by eleven years of war. We must put an end to this."

I shifted restlessly in the carved chair. "I have no love for the Swede," I said, "or for the Emperor. What is it to me who rules Bohemia? My price is gold, nothing more."

Wallenstein watched me closely, pouring out a drop more of the brandy with long, elegant hands. "I have discovered," he said, "that men have more than one price. It occurs to me that there is something for which you might serve more faithfully than for gold."

I laughed. "And what would that be, sir?"

"Land," he said. "Land to call your own, to be your own and your heirs' forever, a hearth to retire to and money to sustain you when you are old." He spread his blue veined hands to the flames. "Believe me, you will be old."

I stared at him, scarcely believing what I heard. Land was of all things the most impossible. I may as well have set my price at a Cardinal's robe.

The Generalissimo continued on as though he had noticed nothing. "Those who serve me well, who are loyal to me, and through me to the Emperor, will be awarded lands of suitable size reclaimed by the Emperor from the rebel lords."

"I see," I said quietly, as unbidden to my mind came the picture of green hills, herds of grazing horses, church towers against the morning sky. There was a sword blade between me and them.

"Those who serve me faithfully," Wallenstein said.

"I am your true man," I replied. "My word is my bond."

"I would not have your bond," the old man said. "Hope of reward is better than any bond. Instead, I hold out to you this hope, and I give you command over two other companies besides your own. I have work for you, Captain."

We met General von Mansfeld at Dessau in April, a deathtrap on the Elbe River, the acrid cannon smoke yellow against the fog. The fight was like a dream, scattered impressions of entrails in the mud, yellow streaks in the sky, and the booming of our guns.

I took a musket ball through the left thigh, shattering the bone just below the socket. My Second, a Scotsman named McDonald, stood the surgeons off with a knife when they tried to amputate, so I did not die, but the bone set wrong, leaving me with a pit in my thigh the size of a plum and a ragged, ugly limp that would last me the rest of my life.

It was nearly a year before I could walk again, and two before I could fight at all on foot. I learned to carry my authority from the saddle, as Wallenstein had made me a colonel when it was certain that I would live.

My hair and beard were streaked with white now, but my spurs were gilded and my doublet was of black velvet, with wide falls of lace at the throat. I commanded eight hundred men in the service of the Holy Roman Emperor.

Nineteen years had passed. In the spring of 1633 the tide of war again turned to Bohemia, and with the spring came my orders and dispatches. There, above Wallenstein's signature was the phrase. "In order to secure supply lines in our rear, and to break rebel support in the upcountry, you are hereby ordered to use whatever force you deem necessary to take the fortress of Falkenau."

The old lord of Falkenau was long dead, and the lands had passed to a distant cousin, Lord Jindrich, who was married to the old lord's daughter. They were Protestant, and Jindrich had led troops in rebellion against the Emperor. It was certainly well within our rights to attack the castle.

And so I came back to Falkenau in blazing summer heat, fighting our way up that long valley inch by bloody inch, resisted by more troops than I thought existed in that part of Bohemia. They attacked us encamped and melted away in daylight. Caltrips slowed our cavalry. Archers harassed us. Horses were hamstrung in the picket lines at night.

All summer long, casualty by casualty, foul well by foul well, we fought beneath snow-topped mountains, while untouched and serene the fortress of Falkenau floated like a dream on a cloud. I do not know how many farmers' sons from Saxony and Poland looked on it as their last sight. I was ready to raze it to the ground.

Week after week the dispatches were more insistent. "Why haven't you taken Falkenau?"

"This Lord Jindrich," I wrote back, "Does not fight like the gentleman we have been led to believe he is. He fights like a bandit, always striking at us from cover, using the terrain to his advantage, drawing us into poor positions."

Wallenstein's answer was brief. "Gain the advantage." He also sent three artillery pieces and a company of sappers.

In August we were before Falkenau. I had replacements up from Prague, which was good, as I had lost two hundred men in this cursed valley. "Take the fortress without delay," Wallenstein instructed.

A week later I wrote back by the light of one of the last tallow candles in the valley, alone at night in my tent, listening to the moans of my wounded. "The walls of Falkenau are twenty-five feet thick. The defenders are well-armed, and do not hesitate to make use of archaic weaponry like the crossbow if they think it is to their advantage. Today three of my men were seriously injured by a fall of boiling oil. The townspeople and farmers are against us, and I do not dare send a foraging party of less than fifty, as they do not return. Lord Jindrich has turned his peasants into soldiers."

Wallenstein's reply was succinct. "Turn your soldiers into soldiers and take Falkenau."

September came. The sappers blew a hole in the curtain wall with a huge charge of gunpowder. On a bright day smelling of autumn and powder smoke, a flag of truce hung from the walls of Falkenau.

An old guardsman with his arm in a sling came out to talk to us, picking his way over the piles of rubble. High above, on the castle walls where the freshening wind blew hair and cloaks back like pennants, half the still-living garrison waited. The guardsman looked uncertainly from McDonald in his splendid plumed hat to me on my white Andalusian.

"I am in charge here," I said, the wind carrying my words

away. "Captain Von Marianburg. You may address yourself to me."

He looked up at me warily while I held Xavier in sharp check. "I've come to ask your terms for surrender."

Beside me McDonald took a deep breath.

"My terms are these," I said. "Falkenau and its defenders are to surrender to the Holy Roman Emperor, represented by his Generalissimo Von Wallenstein and by me. Falkenau and its contents are upon the mercy of the crown, and at their disposal." I raised my voice over the rising wind. "The Lord Jindrich is to surrender to me personally, alone."

"But . . ." the man began.

"Those are the Emperor's terms," I snapped. "Take them, or I will raze every stone to the foundations!" I wheeled Xavier and turned my back on him.

McDonald pulled up beside me as the man made his way back inside the fortress. "Do you think they'll take it?"

"They'd better," I said. "For four months they've been lucky. I'm out of patience with it. We've been tied up here too long."

It was not long before an answer came.

For the first time in months the gates of Falkenau opened. We waited.

Out of the shadow of the gatehouse they walked slowly, a woman in a black dress leading a little boy by the hand, the nurse behind with a babe in arms. They walked carefully, keeping pace with the three-year-old's small steps, the woman's hair and clothes covered with black veils, the color of mourning.

McDonald said something under his breath, but I did not hear him. The child's eyes were huge and dark, but he walked straight ahead holding onto his mother's hand. The wind stirred her clothes, her old fashioned square necked dress, and sent her veil flying out behind her like a banner, exposing the white line of her throat and her smooth red-bronze hair. She lifted her head then and did not look away.

Blue eyes, I thought, more angry than frightened. She crossed the distance between us, and as I cursed and tried to pull Xavier in, she dragged the child to his knees beside her in the dirt almost beneath the Andalusian's hooves, the old black velvet billowing out around her.

Xavier went up on two legs. I hauled him in, pulling him hard to the right, away from the child's bared and lowered head.

"Where is your husband, Lady?" I demanded, calming Xavier to a nervous dance.

Her voice was clear above the wind. "My lord husband was killed in April last, fighting for his King." She gestured to the child at her left hand. "This is my son, the Lord Jindrich. The babe you see is his brother, Karl. I am Izabela, the Lady of Falkenau." There was a tremor in her voice but it was still strong and carried to my men. "I surrender the fortress to you."

You surrender nothing, Lady, I thought. You come before my men in your pride and your beauty to shame them that it has taken four months for Wallenstein's finest to subdue peasants, a woman, and two babes.

"You do not know mercenaries, madam," I snapped. "Let us have no more of this display unless you would have rape and butchery within the castle walls." She paled a little at that, and I went on in a lower tone. "My men have been four months outside the gates of Falkenau. They think nothing of your pride, and as for your pretty children, they would as soon split their heads open as look at them. Have you gold in Falkenau?"

She hesitated, and I leaned down to her. "Speak quickly, lady, as I have six hundred dogs on a single leash."

She looked away. "There is some still. Only about 9,000 kroner."

I did the math quickly in my head, rose in my stirrups so that they could all see me. "Men of Von Marianburg's Company!" I shouted. "The Lady Izabela of Falkenau has surrendered the fortress and agrees to pay a bounty for its ransom! Every man here is to have ten gold kroner from the treasury of Falkenau!"

Their shout echoed off the gully and the stone walls before us.

"Marianburg! Marianburg!"

"In addition," I shouted, "We shall provision ourselves from their stores!"

Izabela's head shot up defiantly, but she said nothing.

"There will be," I continued, "no further looting or harassment of the populace, as this is now the property of the Emperor. Rape and pillage shall be rewarded with hanging. Do I make myself clear?"

Silence reigned all around, broken by a little grumbling.

"Ten gold kroner a man, as bounty for the fortress!" I shouted, "And the beef and wine of Falkenau!"

They cheered me again, raucous this time.

"McDonald, have the 1st company stand down from arms," I said. I looked down at Izabela. She looked ill. "Lady, give me your hand."

For a moment I thought she would not, but then she raised her chin and put her hand in mine, and I raised her to her feet while the soldiers cheered around us, and at last I came in to Falkenau.

The interior of the fortress was a mess, as might be expected after weeks of siege. The great hall stank of peasants and their livestock, too many human and animal bodies in too small a space.

"These peasants are to be returned to their homes," I directed. "And the great hall is to be made habitable for a company of my men. The rest are to be lodged in the village. You will see to that, McDonald. The Lady Izabela will continue in her duties as chatelaine unless I have reason to remove her." I turned to the young woman in her old black dress. "Do not give me reason to remove you. It will go easier on your people under your supervision than mine." She nodded shortly, but I could see the taut fury in her face. "Lady," I said more quietly, "Do not even think of poison. I am the only thing that stands between you and worse. I will not loot this castle because it is of more worth to the Emperor intact than carried off piecemeal in rucksacks." I looked her up and down coldly. "And you are worth more to me as chatelaine than as whore. I am more interested in your spreading acres than your spread legs. The next captain might not feel the same."

I turned away, but not before I saw the flush of humiliation mount in her face. As well, I thought. If this is not taken firmly in hand at the first there will be no controlling her, and I would rather have humiliation than bloodshed. Especially my own blood shed. She was not above poison.

"You, your children and your ladies will continue to occupy your quarters. I would advise you to remain in them when not engaged in the business of running the castle. Chambers will be prepared for me and my officers. You will place at my disposal the rooms belonging to your late husband."

"It will be done," she said, tight-lipped.

It was. The chamber was in the westward tower, looking out over the valley, just at the corner where the tower joined the keep. It had a huge fireplace, louvers on the windows, Flemish tapestries of a stag hunt, and an enormous carven bed draped in green velvet. There was a table for my maps and papers, a leather chair, and a twisted iron floor stand to hold candles. I walked to the windows in the autumn afternoon and looked out across the chasm and the valley at the haze of colored mountains, the faint wreath of smoke that drifted like a dream across the river.

There had been lights in this room nineteen years ago when I was a penniless boy and Izabela a babe in her cradle. She was born under the midwinter sign of Capricorn, a fire in the dead of winter's cold with flame colored hair.

In the great chair of the old lord I wrote a letter to Wallenstein. "I have taken the fortress of Falkenau."

The peace lasted six days. My men were quartered in the town and castle well enough. Food would be short for everyone in the valley this winter because of the interrupted harvest. Two of my men were flogged for stealing chickens, but other than that it was quiet, until the night Izabela tried to murder me.

The room I had been given had only one door, which I kept bolted on the inside while I slept, as mercenaries are not trusting sorts. I could not go to sleep until late, however, so I had only just banked the fire, blown out the candles and gone to bed when I heard a soft click. I did not open my eyes, only looked out from beneath the lashes as a panel in the eastward wall slid open on well-oiled hinges.

With no light to guide her it was dark as the tomb. I could see the faint white shape of her nightdress, and I cursed myself for not wondering if this castle did not have, as so many did, a private passageway connecting the apartments of lord and lady.

I didn't wonder for more than a second who my visitor was

or what she wanted. I heard her listen to my even, sleeping breathing, heard the soft sound of the knife sliding clear of the scabbard. Two footsteps.

Just before she landed on me I rolled to the side, the dagger sinking deep into the pillow, a cloud of feathers flying up. She twisted, but I had her wrist in my right hand and the heavy bed covers impeded her. She fought like a cat, twisting beneath me as I pinned her with my weight, bending her knife hand further and further back.

"Do I have to break your wrist?" I said, jerking her by her long hair with my other hand and turning up her face to mine.

Her knife hand unclenched, and I grabbed the dagger, throwing it back over my shoulder toward the fireplace.

She bit my wrist hard enough to draw blood, and I hit her open-handed in the side of the head as she kicked and writhed beneath me.

"I will not have this, madam," I panted.

She looked up at me and I thought it was the moment where she would either spit in my face or burst into tears. Izabela did neither. She just looked at me with an expression that was quizzical and completely unafraid, her long slim legs wrapped around my body. I was not prepared for what I wanted, and there were no knives in it.

I stood up, jerking her to her feet, all disheveled hair and torn nightdress. "Go to your chambers, madam," I rasped, and turned my back on her.

For a moment there was silence, then the sound of the panel closing. I went to the fireplace and retrieved the dagger, but I did not put the clothes press in front of the secret door.

On the morrow she was cool as ice, but in the next days as our business brought us together, as it often did, I would catch her watching me warily and curiously, as though I were some strange beast she had not seen before.

Five days after two of my men killed a farmer and his wife who would not tell them where their money was hidden. Naturally the first I heard of it was from Izabela. She came upon me in the great hall before two dozen of my men as I was hearing the reports of the sentries I had placed.

"Captain Von Marianburg!" she demanded, striding into the hall in a movement of dusty black velvet, her bailiff at her elbow. "There is a matter which requires your attention most urgently."

I turned a little impatiently. She had two of my men with her, a sergeant, and half a dozen peasants. Izabela's eyes were snapping. She gestured to the two men under the sergeant's guard. "These men killed one of my farmers and his wife. Here are the witnesses."

The men scowled as her peasants began the story in their own tongue, not a word of German between them, but I had been long in Bohemia. When they finished I asked the sergeant, "Is what they say true?"

The sergeant shuffled his feet. "As far as I know. This one admitted to knifing the old man."

I nodded. "Take them out into the courtyard," I said to McDonald. "And hang them."

He took them out while Izabela watched with unholy joy.

"Come, madam," I said quietly. "You can watch what is wrought in your name."

"With a great will," she said.

One of them begged for mercy and the other did not. I stood and watched while the ropes were put around their necks, while they dangled kicking as they strangled, and smiled all the while not because I wished to but because I must seem the kind of man who took pleasure in such things.

When they were dead and cut down I went back inside. A courier had come with a dispatch from Wallenstein in Plzen. It was direct and to the point, commending me in the name of the Emperor for the capture of Falkenau and instructing me to use the castle and its lands for winter quarters. It wasn't until I reached the last page that my blood ran cold.

"In reward for your good service, and to strengthen your base of operations in the area, you are instructed without delay to marry the Lady Izabela of Falkenau."

Izabela took the news with surprising calm. She sat sewing in her rooms, the children's nurse nearby with her charges lest it be thought I planned to consummate it forthwith. Izabela laid the fragile embroidered rose aside as I read Wallenstein's letter, and I did not look at her face, only at the white rose picked out in silk on damask.

I finished the letter and put it away. "Believe me, madam," I said. "This was not my idea."

"I believe you, Captain," she said, her lips thinning. "You have already made your disdain for my person abundantly clear."

"As clear as your marked distaste of mine," I replied. Even in the old black dress she was uncommonly beautiful.

"Well?" said Izabela. "Are you going to ask for my hand or just demand it?"

She would love it, I thought, for me to go down on one knee when I could hardly do so with any grace, a man decades her elder on his knees to his betters. I would make a pretty fool of myself. "Just demand it, madam," I replied, not sounding as harsh as I wished.

Izabela folded her hands. "I see. Then I have only one request."

"What is that?" I asked.

"That the service be performed by a Protestant minister." Her eyes met mine, perfectly level and grave. "It is enough that I am forced to marry a man who has despoiled my lands and people without being forced into a state of concubinage by the officiation of a priest I do not recognize and the authority of a Pope I do not acknowledge!"

I stared at her speechless. "It is all one to me," I managed. "I care not if we are married by priest, minister, or a devil of the South Seas. If it would ease your conscience or make you an obedient wife to me, then you may have your Lutheran minister."

Izabela did not look away from me. "I thank you for that, Captain. However, the devil himself could not make me an obedient wife to you."

"Then you may find, madam, that I can be the very devil himself."

"I am sure you can be, Captain," she replied. "I am quite certain you are capable of beating into submission a helpless woman with no one to turn to and two babies to shelter."

"Your frailty seems to come and go when it is convenient to you," I remarked. "You did not seem so fragile the other night."

Izabela looked at me for a long moment and then dropped her eyes in a submissive gesture I did not believe for an instant. "As my lord wishes," she said.

She had her Protestant minister, the same one from the village church who had married her to Lord Jindrich five years before. My Second, McDonald, stood up with me in the old chapel of Falkenau. Izabela wore black. So did I, unrelieved by any ornament except a wealth of lace at throat and cuffs. The minister was nervous, unwilling, and at one point stopped altogether.

"Go on," Izabela said softly.

The minister cleared his throat. "Do you, Izabela Maria Oriana, take this man, Georg von Marianburg of the Imperial Army, as your lawful husband, to have and to hold, to cherish and obey, from this day forward, until death do you part?"

Her voice was clear and strong. "I do."

I do not remember my responses, only the look of surprised on her face when I put on her finger my heavy ring of rubies and pearls. To my mind the ceremony was too plain, with no incense, no vestments, no choir, but I could not fault the beauty of the bride. The black dress was no doubt meant as an insult, but I had foreseen that, and my black velvet matched hers. Instead of clashing we looked as though we belonged together, for all that she was young and lovely as a candle flame. I was the shadow to that flame, austere and solid as the stones of Falkenau around us.

Her lips, when I bent to kiss them, were still and cool as a statue's.

I took her upstairs myself after what passed for a wedding supper, instead of leaving her to the care of her women as is proper. I was afraid there would be more knives, or perhaps a flying leap out the window. More likely knives. I could not imagine Izabela taking the coward's way out.

My men yelled the usual rowdy jokes at us, nothing unusual in a crowd of mercenaries, but Izabela's jaw was clenched tight. I laughed and assured them that I meant to plow my field well, and did not let go the grip I had gotten on her arm. I felt it tremble a little as we mounted the stairs and I thought there was the fear at last, the fear of my hands and what will come after. Her hair was like a living flame as she walked ahead of me. I was more cheerful and more pleased by good wine than was my usual nature, and it seemed to me there was nothing more perfect than the fine, thin bones at the back of her neck and the white unbruised skin. I closed the door behind us.

I stood some little time thus, with my back to her as I removed my sash and lace neckcloth and sable gloves. I would make a wedding gift of her modesty.

I turned about at last. She stood beside the great bed clad in nothing but her glorious hair, and that she had left pinned up that it might veil nothing. Even her hands she held away from her sides. "See, my lord?" she inquired sarcastically. "What a bargain you have made?" She rotated slowly for my perusal, more beautiful than I had hoped and twice as venomous, holding her hands above her head as though held by invisible fetters. "Is Your Magnificence pleased with your purchase?"

"Madam, so help me," I managed, but the words stuck in my throat. I crossed the room to her. "I will have no more of this!"

"Perhaps I should get right to the point," she hissed, flinging herself backwards on the bed with her legs akimbo, her privates exposed in a manner that would humiliate a town harlot, her hands still held by invisible cords.

I seized her wrists and prized them apart. Her eyes were still snapping hatred, one perfect breast against my knee. "Madam," I said, "A less temperate man would stick a knife in you and be well rid."

"Oh, stick a knife in me!" she spat, but her eyes said something else. "Monster!" she hissed, her wrists gathered in my hand, pressed beneath my weight. "You don't dare!" she whispered. "Or are you gelded too?" And in that moment I perceived the war within her. She would make it rape so that she yielded nothing. Anything less would be surrender.

"Izabela," I said, and laid my hand along the side of her face.

She closed her eyes and was perfectly still. I do not think she moved until she heard me open and close the door of the press away across the room.

"What are you doing?" I heard her ask behind me.

I took off each boot carefully without looking at her. "I am going to bed. Put on your night robe, madam, and spare us any further vulgar scenes." My voice was not as hard as I had meant it, only tired. It would not have gone amiss for once in my life for something to live up to its promise.

I heard her scramble for her night robe among the bedcovers. "I will be going then," she said.

"You will not." I turned to face her. "You will not leave this chamber until morning, not if you spend it tied spreadeagled between the bedposts in the manner you have so well demonstrated." If she left now my men could only come to one conclusion, and it was one that would not serve me well.

She held her robe before her now so that only her shoulders and wild eyes gleamed in the light. "You wouldn't dare!"

"Try me, madam," I said quietly.

She shrugged and pulled her robe over her head.

"You have your choice," I said. "You may pass the night between the posts or at my side as a wife should." I sat down on the side of the bed, undressing as calmly as if I were alone.

Her hair was escaping from its pins, and red-gold frizzles made a bronze halo around her head. "You shall not win my gratitude, Captain. Nor my love."

I meant to say that I had no use for either, but what I said as I snuffed the candle and plunged the room into darkness was, "Izabela, there is nothing I have ever loved that is within your reach." I lay down and turned on my side with my back to my wife.

She sat perfectly still in the dark for a long time. I do not know when she lay down, as I went to sleep.

In the morning she was curled against my back like a kitten in the chill of the room and did not even stir when I got up and left, going downstairs to review the morning dispatches and breakfast with my men. I was glad that she was a widow. If blood on the sheets were required, I was certain there would have been a quantity of it, but hers or mine I could not tell.

But I had many things to think about besides my wife. October turned into November, and the first icy weather blew in, silvering the roofs of Falkenau with icicles that glittered like glass in the morning. With them came a summons to Plzen, where Wallenstein had gone into winter quarters, there to report in person.

It was not so very far, but the weather made the journey unenviable. I cautioned McDonald to take care where the Lady Izabela was concerned, and cautioned her that his temper was much more uncertain than mine, though I did not think she believed me. McDonald would hesitate to beat my wife, if for no other reason than the grave insult to his superior. So it was with vast trepidation about what I should find when I returned that I decamped for Plzen.

I was not surprised that the first person I saw when I arrived was Count Trcka, striding across the courtyard to me before the groom had even taken my horse. "Marianburg!"

"Count," I said, bowing very properly as one should.

"None of that," he said, and put his arm about my shoulders. "You're a landed gentleman now. Congratulations on your marriage!"

"Thank you," I said. It had not quite occurred to me that

I was now Graf Falkenau. The castle and title were Izabela's inheritance, and unless they should pass to the sons of her first marriage . . . .

"I hear she's a pretty thing." Trcka winked at me. He was a large man of my own age with carefully trimmed dark hair and beard and a mobile face that somehow rendered him Gallic in appearance, though he was Bohemian through and through. In his scarlet pantaloons and broad sleeves he was not a sight one could miss.

"She is that," I said, and steered the conversation onto other courses before the subject of the marriage's consummation arose. "What does the Generalissimo want with me? To remonstrate about how long this took?"

Trcka waved it away. "Nonsense. He was busy all fall himself. So were we all. No, rather you are here at my wish."

I frowned. I'd fought beside Trcka many times in the last decade, and might even call him friend, but the orders had come under Wallenstein's seal. Still, Wallenstein was his brother in law, as they'd married landed sisters together, Wallenstein the elder and Trcka the younger. "What do you need me for?" I asked.

"We'll talk of it later." Adam Trcka clapped me on the shoulder and released me. "My man will show you to comfortable quarters. Dine with me and we'll discuss it all."

"Of course," I said a little stiffly.

He shook his head, smiling. "Same old Marianburg. Suspicious and without humor. Cannot you believe in good fortune?"

"As much as any man," I said.

"A sober fellow," he said. "We'll talk later." And he left me with that.

I was not reassured. After all, not everything he had suggested in the past had turned out well, case in point one particular evening before the Battle of Lutzen.

I would never have considered doing it at all if it weren't for a large quantity of excellent Polish vodka. I do not believe in spirits, let alone believe that men may congress with them aided by candles and chalk. Trcka believed differently, as did McDonald.

"Come, Georg," McDonald said, reeling a little from the drink, "I've stood at your back often enough. Stand at mine, so that if demons attempt me it may be your swift knife!"

"There are no such things as demons," I said testily.

"We aren't summoning demons," Trcka said. "That's a dangerous business and I'll have none of it. We're summoning angels, that they may tell us the fates of our battles in the coming days. One angel in particular, the Archangel Michael, who watches over war."

"Come, Georg," McDonald said. "If you have nothing to fear, why do you hesitate?"

"I fear that in your drunk clumsiness you will set your hair afire or your beard or the table," I said, but came with them to the upper room of the inn we had appropriated. Appropriated–pillaged rather, along with the good vodka and a quantity of Rhenish wine.

Trcka chalked the circles and walked them round, telling McDonald and me where to stand, setting candles on the tables, on the window sill. Most of what he said was gibberish to me. Perhaps it was Greek, or some more archaic tongue. I wouldn't know. I am not a learned man. I stood there where Trcka told me while he poured out wine, drew his sword and chanted out a great many words, walking round and round about inside his circle of chalk.

Perhaps I should have been afraid. Most would be. This was, after all, black magic proscribed by Church and Emperor alike. It was death to begin this, or at least it would be so for those without wealth and rank to protect them. If I feared anything it was this, not imaginary demons from some medieval bestiary, the imaginings of monks with nothing better to amuse themselves.

McDonald sat down on the floor. "Are you all right, James?" I asked.

"Sleepy, so sleepy," he said, leaning back against the wall.

"You're dead drunk," I said.

"Mmmmm," he murmured.

I shrugged. He could sleep there against the wall and no harm would come to him. I spread his cloak over him.

When I looked up, Trcka had stopped pacing and mumbling. He slumped in a chair, his eyes closed, the chalk dangling from one hand, the sword from the other. I stepped over to him. He was snoring softly.

I was a bit unsteady on my feet myself. "Vodka," I said. "Plays tricks on you." This seemed terribly profound to me. "Sleep it off then. A quiet end to this charade." Nothing whatsoever had happened.

I went over and blew out the candle at the window sill. In the sudden burst of light as the flame was extinguished I saw the reflection of the fourth man. I would have thought it was one of our troopers, except for the shadow of folded wings behind him, cast high on the wall.

I turned.

He wore bloodstained velvet and a breastplate of good Spanish steel, light brown hair framing a tired young face, lined with care and weal. A blackened swept hilt rapier was at his side. His voice was very cool. "You should have a care, summoning your betters. It's not polite."

"My Lord," I said, "I do not believe in you."

Something moved in his eyes, some expression of regret. "Do you not?" he said, "Son of my heart? Can you have forgotten yourself so much?"

"I have forgotten nothing," I said, and a great anger rose in me, the battle blindness I sometimes feel, pure and hot as fire. "Where were you when my stepfather beat me bloody again and again? Where were you when his fists blinded my mother and broke her jaw? When I killed him as he stood, when I was fifteen, and still she wept and said that she should turn me over to the Graf's men for a murderer so that I should hang for killing him? Where were you when I fled from that place with nothing but my shirt and a bloody knife to make my way in this world?" I turned away from him. "I would that you were more than drunken imaginings so that I might put this blade through you."

He stepped around the table, the feathers of his wings rippling softly. He stood very close, and there seemed little celestial about him, just a man of my own age, tired and sleepless. "Do you think I would not prevent such things if I could? I would that I could, that infinite power were mine. But if it were, I should use it no more wisely than you."

"I do not care for celestial power," I said. "What I want is money, a good sword and men to follow after me."

"So that no one may harm you," he said.

"Yes!" I spat it at him. "You have named it. There is no mercy in this fallen world, and I shall show none. Perhaps I am a beaten cur, hard bitten and hard biting. But if you had wished otherwise, you could have shown yourself twenty years ago!"

His eyes searched my face. "Mercenary captain. Who would have thought that you would even survive this long? Much less stand with lace at your throat and two hundred horsemen at your back?"

"I'm hard to kill, My Lord."

"I know." The angel almost smiled. "You stand there in black velvet, unbowed still. Perhaps there is some hope left in this bleeding continent. Have you never believed in anything?"

I sat down at the table heavily. Trcka slumbered on in the chair beside me. "I believed in the Winter Queen," I said. "But she was dross. She and her king fled, and left us to die on the mountain covering her retreat. So I fight no more for queens or thrones. I serve Wallenstein, who pays in gold. I care not for Emperor or Pope or kings." I looked up at him.

"You have come so far," he said, his eyes searching my face, "from that bright girl alive with hope. So far from those days when even I was young. The world is older, now, and a new dark age upon us. This land is drowning in blood, and I do not see the end of it."

"You tell me what I know," I said. "Now the kings of Sweden and France enter in, and there is no end to war."

"Yet you live," he said, and took a breath. "I shall take some hope in that. That battered and changed, you endure. And perhaps you will find your way back from these caves. I cannot tell."

"My Lord," I said, "What will be our fortunes in the field?"

The angel gave a rueful smile. "I can tell you nothing you do not know. You will meet the King of Sweden in battle, and many brave men will die. You will win, or they will. And whoever prevails will fight again and again."

"Will I die, My Lord?" I asked.

"No," Michael said. "That would be too easy."

I had not spoken of these things to Trcka, nor would I. When I had awakened in the morning it seemed little more than a foul dream brought on by drink and atmosphere. And yet I was quite certain that I never wanted to do such things again. If something of the kind was the reason he had summoned me to Plzen I resolved to refuse even if it were grave disrespect.

Our meal was served privately in an upper room, well seasoned fresh cutlets of pork and a dish of stewed apples, sweet Rhenish wine and a pastry thick with almond paste, and brandy to follow. It was very good.

"Did it ever occur to you," Trcka asked at last, dabbing at the marzipan in his moustache, "that there are other ways to live?"

"It occurs to me constantly," I said dryly. How not? Trcka should eat well if it were the last pig in Bohemia, and perhaps it was, so ruined was the countryside from fifteen years of war. I had not eaten thus in my childhood, when a sausage was dinner for us all, and a grand one at that with some cabbage. At Falkenau the winter would be harsh, but with care we might all see spring. If I were strict enough with the food now and let no man eat his fill, including myself.

Trcka laughed as though I had made some great piece of wit. "I don't mean the food," he said, and his eyes were sober over his glass. "The ancients did not live thus. Pax Romana, Roman peace, enduring centuries from one end of the world to the other. They built roads and temples and towns, bridges that endure today! In Italy where are waterworks that still faithfully bring water from artesian springs into cities, fresh and pure as mountain air!"

"What is all that to me?" I asked.

"I thought you of all people had the imagination to think," Trcka said. "What might we do if this war were ended?"

I shrugged. "I don't know." It made me angry for reasons I could not fathom and did not wish to.

"Then what will happen if it does not?" he asked softly. "Surely you can see that."

"There will be nothing left," I said, and I knew what I spoke of. I had seen the smoking ruins with no one left alive, the frightened people taking to the road looking for a safe place when there is none, their screams when cavalry cut through them, riding down children for sport. "There will be nothing," I said. Orchards ablaze, apple blossoms standing for a moment incongruous against the flames before the darkness took them, fields unplowed that would yield no harvest except skeletons, smoke rising to the sky from the pyre of the world.

"No planting and no harvest," Trcka said.

No glass blown in empty shops, a fine pulverized powder all that was left of a craftsman's life, book pages twisting on the wind, torn and worthless and ultimately empty. . . .

"No learning and no printing, no building and no crafting." Trcka put his hands together around his brandy. "We will make a wasteland. We already do."

The words came unbidden in my mind, like words of a song I had heard in childhood. "Who will plant young olive trees? Who will plow fields that are fallow?"

"You will," Trcka said, and his words fell like the bronze tolling of a bell in the silence.

I looked at him, this ordinary man with his ordinary face. "I am a soldier," I said.

He spread his hands. "Let me show you something," he said.

He got up and went to the press, returned with papers that he spread before me. "You read well enough." He opened the first and smoothed it before me. "This was from a courier intercepted in the spring. The second was from one taken in September. I need not tell you their importance."

I read them. I read them twice, turning the pages with careful hands.

"This is a letter," I said, "from Cardinal Richelieu to the Emperor."

"Just so," Trcka said. "From that Richelieu who rules France in all but name. To our Emperor."

"He offers money," I said, reading it again. "A great deal of money. And by the second one it has been accepted, one Catholic monarch to another. Money and guns. Money and cannon." I looked up at Trcka, who bent over the table. "France is allied with the Swedes against us. They have already given them a great deal, otherwise they would have already withdrawn to their own country. Richelieu has been the prop of their army for the last four years."

"And so?" Trcka asked.

"And now he would secretly support us?" Wheels within wheels, a game I could parse too easily. Far too easily.

"What does he gain by that?" Trcka asked quietly.

"You know well what he does," I said. My mouth compressed into a thin line. "He pays us to fight one another. We dance like puppets on a string for his amusement. No, not for his amusement, but for the good of France. Sweden and Bohemia and Poland and all the states of the Empire tear one another apart like dogs in a fight, while France stands back unsullied, her wealth and her palaces intact. He goads us to attack one another, to destroy our universities and kill our farmers, and all it costs him is a bit of gold!"

Trcka nodded.

"We are played for fools," I said. My mind should not compass this, but it too easily did. "Richelieu has played us all for fools. We have spent a decade and more killing one another, Catholic and Protestant alike in the name of God, and it is nothing but Richelieu's game." I looked up at him. "Wallenstein knows?"

"Wallenstein knows," Trcka said. "He gave me leave to speak to you."

I blinked. I said the first thing that came to mind. "Why?"

"Because he seeks a separate peace with the Swedes, and you are his man, not the Emperor's."

I let out a long breath. "That is true," I said. Wallenstein was a soldier and a good one, and I had not met Ferdinand. He did not sully his hands with the likes of me.

"Will you support him?"

"Yes." I looked down at the paper again, proof of the greatest treason. Yes, we were but playthings for the great, but this . . . "What if the king served the country, rather than the country the king?" I said.

"What, indeed?" Trcka smiled. "What if one could trade a bad king for a better?"

"That is indeed treason," I said, but there was no heat in it. The Emperor was elected from among the nobles. Why not a good rather than a bad? Emperors had been deposed before.

"Perhaps the Emperor will see reason," Trcka said. "After all, Wallenstein has an army, and he does not."

"Perhaps he will," I said. It would take an army to countermand the effects of Richelieu's gold. A man could live in exile very comfortably for the rest of his life on a tenth of it, or spend his days in pampered splendor at the Luxembourg. I stood and gave Trcka my hand. "I will stand with you," I said.

I returned to Falkenau on a late autumn day when the wind blew gusts around the towers, dead leaves chasing each other like goats on the mountains. Cloaked and muffled, we got in ahead of the rain. I was unsurprised to find my wife on the walls of Falkenau, looking north and west into the storm. The freshening wind was laden with moisture, and her hair whipped in fine strands about her face like red gold against a sky of gray.

"What misfortune have you brought today?" Izabela asked me.

"Would that I could tell you," I said. I put my hands upon the parapet and looked out at mountains and sky and all. I had thought this might be mine, but a sword blade still stood between me and it, the treachery of kings.

And yet, that orchard yonder might be replanted. Apples would bear before too long, were there young trees transplanted from another. Those fields had nothing wrong with them, merely the grain burned standing. In the spring the stubble could be plowed under and the field would be as rich as ever. Soon winter would come and water it all, cover everything beneath a pall of snow. We would be short of supplies, but there was enough, I thought. Barely enough. And then spring would come with her healing cloak of green.

If this were mine I should love it with all my heart. I should know it, each stone and each tree, each bridge and each well, the shape of each far peak against the sky seen only as they are from Falkenau. When I die, my bones should molder here, becoming one with this land, a bit of me passing into dirt and leaf and tree, a tie that could not be broken though centuries should pass.

Izabela was looking at me sideways, a strange expression on her face.

"Politics, madam," I said. No doubt it would please her to know that the Catholic Emperor was false to his own. But the Protestant princes were no better. They too were Richelieu's dupes.

"Why did you ask for the minister?" I asked, and added at her blank look, "rather than a priest?"

"Because I am Protestant," she said, as though that were obvious.

I shook my head. There was a faint spatter of freckles on Izabela's nose courtesy of the summer sun that now faded from the sky. "And that matters to you?"

"Yes." Izabela folded her hands on the stone, lifting her face to the wind. The sky had darkened with the clouds and coming night. "I believe that every man and every woman comes before God on his or her own merits with no interventions, no dispensations and no allowances, with no witness to speak for them save their own deeds. And I believe that God speaks to each of us as He wills. We do not need a priest to stand intermediary between us and God, for we are each a precious child of His own creation."

"Born in sin to die in sin," I said.

"And yet through our actions are we redeemed, and by our faith saved," Izabela said. There was a curious smile on her face, as though her skin was but a vessel for something luminous. "Mine is not the God of fires and pits, but the God who so loved the world that He gave his only begotten son, that whosoever believes in Him may not perish but have everlasting life." She turned her eyes to mine. "I did not understand that until I had sons of my own. To give your own child, to give your own sweet son . . .

What love could be so strong that one would do so?"

"I don't know," I said.

Something in her face closed. "And you will take my sons from me when you wish. Do you think I do not know that you will kill them?"

I opened my mouth and shut it again.

"If you would have Falkenau pass to the heirs of your body, do you think I do not know what stands in your way?" Her mouth narrowed to a thin line. "They will not be the first boys killed by a murderous stepfather. So you will see that I will do whatever will save them."

"I will do them no harm while you are cooperative," I managed.

She snorted. "And when I have cooperated and you have got another son on me? Do you think I will believe that? Falkenau passes through the heirs of my body, not yours. If you would truly own it, then you know what you must do. And so do I."

"I think that is unlikely," I said. I took a step closer, my side to her, looking into the eye of the north wind. "I will not live so long. What use in begetting a son when the time is already gone? I am not a young man, Izabela, and there are endless battles before me. Chances are I would not see it weaned. In the spring I will be gone to war."

Unless there was peace. Unless Wallenstein traded for peace.

She did not speak, only waited me out. Unless there was a change in the stars, something marked in the wind. Unless the world were transformed. And yet I did not think it would be. I thought there would be war. What use in planting fields that would be trampled before the harvest? What use in begetting children to be tiny corpses at the next turn of the tide?

Whatever I did, it would not matter. And therein lay the crux of it.

I glanced at her sideways, so young and so certain. "Do you never waver in your faith?"

Her eyes slid from mine and she leaned upon her elbows against the wall. The first raindrops spattered around us in a gust of wind. "Sometimes," she said. "I waver." She lifted her face to the rain and did not look at me. "In the spring when my husband died and the armies came down upon us, I prayed to the Archangel Michael to send help not for me, but for my sons and for my people. And instead there was you."

My throat closed and there was nothing I could say. Above, the banners flew in the wind, billowing around the skirts of her black dress as though we were two ravens who perched there, carrion eaters poised above the carnage of the world.

Another spatter of rain, and I took her arm. "Come inside, Izabela," I said. "It is raining."

I went down and found McDonald in the stableyard. "Walk with me," I said.

He followed me through the hall and up the stair, down a winding passage that zigzagged between parts of the castle built in different centuries, to the lord's chamber. I closed the door behind us. He looked at me with a frown. "What's wrong?"

I told him all, Richelieu and the rest, pacing the room like a caged beast, from door to windows that looked on mountains and river.

When I was finished, McDonald sank into my chair beside the map table. "A fine mess," he said. Then he shrugged, eyes very blue. "But what's in it for us? Wallenstein's separate peace, I mean? If he makes peace with the Swedes and Protestants, what becomes of us?"

For a moment I couldn't fathom what he was talking about.

McDonald gestured around the fine room. "It's all well enough for you," he said. "You've got your share. You'll stay here and be Graf Falkenau married to a pretty wench and spend the rest of your life collecting taxes and siring fat children. But what about those boys downstairs? Most of them have never known any life except at arms. They've got no prospects and no crafts. If peace breaks out they've nothing to do except turn bandit. What about your men, Georg? Surely you're not so blinded by the Lady Izabela's spreading acres that you've forgotten about them?"

I drew a deep breath. "You know as well as I that most of them will never have any more land than the grave they lie in. You and I—we're rare birds, Jamie. Old mercenaries. Most of them won't live five years, much less retire rich men."

"But they might. And that's the siren, my friend. You heard her song and so did I. One more battle, one more march, and we'll get our own. Our ships will come in and we'll live on milk and honey. As long as you keep believing it you'll keep fighting." McDonald crossed his legs. "I'm not so much worried for me. I'd make a fine master at arms for Falkenau. But you can't keep them all on. What use is there for a company if peace breaks out?"

"I never believed that," I said sharply. "I never believed there was anything for me except a grave."

McDonald shrugged. "And yet here you are, Graf Falkenau. Mayhap you didn't believe it, but you did it all the same. You've a rare kind of stubbornness to you and a quicksilver wit behind those black Bavarian eyes. I said to myself, there's a man who's lucky, so I'll stand behind him. It's paid off so far. But you know as well as I that fear of you is the only thing that's keeping some of those lads from torching castle and village both." He shook his head. "You can't turn off an army of mercenaries, Georg."

"Don't you think Wallenstein knows that?" I asked. "He's twenty years longer at this game than we, and the canniest man in the empire. If he's seeking terms he has a plan. Perhaps we'll turn this around and attack Richelieu, give him back a bit of what he's handed out." I paced over to the window again. "In which case you've got the company, my friend. I'll take myself out and you'll be captain. And the boys can do as they wish— sign on with you or muster out."

"They'll sign on, most of them," McDonald said. He gave me a gap toothed smile. "You'll retire, and I'm for a field in the Elsass."

"Unless you'd rather be master at arms for Falkenau," I said.

He shook his head. "Not me. I'm a gambling man, Georg. One more throw of the dice to make me king!"

A shiver ran down my spine, as though we had spoken of this before. Perhaps we had, only I did not remember it. "Sometimes it's better to leave the table when you're winning," I said. "To leave off grasping for the ring of fire and be content with what you have, rather than risk all and lose all."

"Maybe so," he said, but when it came to that I thought he would not stay.

Winter came, blowing in on the heels of the storm that had followed me, a hard freeze and a light snow, just enough to coat the cobblestones in the night and give a taste of what was to come. We had problems of fodder, and I sent McDonald around with Izabela's factor to see what they could buy up from outlying farms where our army had not yet been. McDonald didn't ask if he could just take it. After all, I was their overlord now, and stealing from my own peasants would be foolish. It would be stealing from myself.

Advent came, and Christmastide. The cheer was perhaps the ghost of what it would have been in a normal year, but we were settling in to some kind of truce. Izabela's people did not hurry through the hall anymore without speaking, their eyes averted. There were fewer crude jests and more flirtation. I'd hang a man for rape, but a word here and there, a strong back to carry a heavy load of laundry upstairs, a word from a handsome fellow . . . Some would find their Christmas cheer.

Not I. Izabela spent one night in seven in my room for form's sake, lest people talk, but I had not touched her. Usually we did not speak at all, merely slept back to back in the big curtained bed without a word said, our truce in force. And yet during the day I thought we were not so ill-matched. She was clever and quick, and if her reading had not the breadth of mine it had more method. After all, she had been carefully taught from childhood, trained for the responsibilities that would be hers since she was a babe in the cradle.

"Of course I read Latin," she said in surprise one day when I found her bent over a medical book. "And French. And a little Greek, though I had not got much of that before I married." Her voice sounded a little wistful. "My father had no son, and I knew what I must be. He saw me well settled before he died."

"And your husband?" I asked, going about the table she worked at and sitting in a chair where she could keep my hands in view.

"He was my cousin. It was all arranged," Izabela said. Her eyes evaded mine. "He was a good man."

"But you did not love him." The words slipped out before I could stop them.

Izabela smiled at me. "What is love, Captain? I was betrothed to him when I was eight and he fourteen, and we married five years later. It was a good match and it kept the peace between our houses. I could not rule Falkenau alone, and I was born in the twilight of my father's life. He knew he would not live to see his grandchildren and indeed he did not. He died when I was fourteen. How should I have held Falkenau alone, a girl of fourteen with no husband? I should have been prey for any hawk that wanted to stoop upon us. Jindrich brought the protection of his family and his name as well as his sword arm."

"And yet you are the more talented in battle," I said, remembering the defense of Falkenau. That had not been shabby for a woman still short of twenty. Beneath her pretty eyes she was better than I.

"A quirk of fate," Izabela said. She shook her head and for a moment I thought I saw tears there. "Were I a man I could defend my people and my God and would not have to look to such as you."

"True enough," I said. "But does it not stand to reason that your God has made you this way with a purpose?"

"I wish I knew what it was," she said. She looked away. "I see no reason in it, save to teach me humility."

"And have I humbled you so?" I asked. "By God, madam, not half of what I could!"

"Well I know the threat that hangs over me," she retorted.

"Then would it not be better to do it and have done?" I asked. Perhaps my pride smarted. Or perhaps it was desire. "Or is that a field in which you fear to face me?"

"I do not fear anything about you, captain," Izabela said.

Spots of color appeared on her face. Her clear, translucent skin showed everything.

"Then come and give me a kiss," I said.

I expected that she would flounce from the room with a quick riposte, but she did not. Izabela rose from her chair and walked around the table very deliberately. I did not move. I did not twitch a muscle as she bent and touched her lips to mine.

There was fire. She was no timid thing, no trembling virgin scarce touched. Her husband had got two sons on her, and she had enjoyed the making of them from the way she kissed, consumingly and intemperately, as though it were a challenge with trumpets and all, as though it were she who stooped to conquer. It was I who was left breathless as she straightened, the color high in her face.

"I do not fear to meet you, captain," she said.

"Perhaps you might progress to Georg under the circumstances," I managed, thanking whatever demons owned my soul that I had nearly two decades on her in age. Were I a boy her age I should belong to her like a lap dog.

Izabela's eyebrows rose. "Should I seduce you then? Wrap you about my finger and so secure clemency for my people?"

"It is a time-tested strategy," I acknowledged.

Izabela sat down on the edge of the map table, another foot between us, which was probably a mercy. "You do not have the power to grant what I want," she said.

"And what is that?"

"That we should not have to convert or face the sword." Her chin rose. "Your Emperor will make us Catholic. This is Hussite country, Georg. We know what it is to lose. We know what it is to be persecuted for our beliefs."

"Izabela, I care not whether you worship with priest or

minister," I said. "It is all one to me. I care not if you light candles to the Virgin or Baphomet or that ancient fellow Jupiter! Have I raised a hand to stop your pastor from preaching? Even once?"

"You have not," she acknowledged. "And we do know that. But your Emperor will not let it remain so, and you cannot gainsay the powerful men who will require it of you."

"He is not my Emperor," I snapped. "You speak as though I chose him. I have no oaths to him. I have not even laid eyes on him! I am Wallenstein's man, and I will go where he goes." And in that moment I realized I had said too much.

Izabela's eyes narrowed. "By which you mean Wallenstein may yet leave the Emperor," she said quietly.

"You have said it, not I."

She regarded me solemnly. "And if so, you are his man, not the Emperor's?"

"Yes," I said.

Izabela sat back on the edge of the table, her skirts brushing against my legs, but I did not think she even noticed. Her face was abstracted, as though she parsed out some tactical problem. "Why would you do that? Why would he?"

"Because if we do not have peace we will have a wasteland," I said. I did retain enough sense not to mention Richelieu. "Wallenstein is Bohemian. He does not wish to see this land made a desert." I sat up and reached for her hand, taking her fingertips in mine. "Izabela, cannot we have a truce? Our interests run together, so far as they go."

"You want Falkenau." Her eyes met mine solidly.

"Yes," I said, and threw the dice once more. "And you cannot hold it without me. You are talented and you have the tactical sense of a man, but you are right that without a husband to act in your name you will be prey for any hunter, while I need you to have any claim to that which I have taken. If we make common cause, who can stand against us?"

"Only the armies of the world," Izabela said, and there was the devil's smile on her lips.

"Then let the armies of the world try us," I said.

At that she laughed, but she did not withdraw her hand from mine. "You are very strange," she said.

"Am I?"

"Stern and cheerless, but when you say things like that it is almost as if there is someone else inside you, someone I might like to know." She shook her head. "I do not have it in me to fear you."

"Perhaps that is your temper, not mine," I said. "Well, Izabela? A truce between us?"

"A truce," she said. "And let it serve as it may."

Winter came down in earnest. The mountain roads were clogged with snow. It took three days for a dispatch rider to reach Plzen, a distance that was only a day in good weather. February opened, candles for the Churching of the Virgin glimmering on the snow, a hard freeze on top of snow knee deep. The roads closed entirely.

For all practical purposes we were alone. Falkenau might have been the only settlement of humans in a world of ice. The river was frozen. Snow rested on the ice like a great plowed field. Beneath it, water flowed, cold and ready to swallow the unwary.

There was food enough, carefully rationed out. No roaring fires or roasted boar, but endless cauldrons of soup flavored with a little ham, breakfasts of bread and cheese. We did not live well, but none of us would die. The world narrowed.

And yet somewhere beyond this, beyond the mountains,

things were happening. The occasional dispatch was unenlightening, and yet they left me oddly on edge. They said too little and nothing directly. I should go to Plzen myself and see what passed, but the snow was deep and I had not been ordered to. And yet as the days passed, as February began to wane, a deep unease settled over me.

Perhaps it is only the weather, I thought. Perhaps it will break with the thaw. Already the days grew longer, a promise of winter's end.

I dreamed in the bed beside Izabela. I dreamed that I went to report in Plzen and found no one there. Windows were open to the storm, dispatches blowing in the empty rooms. I went to the window and looked out into the snow-wracked darkness. Where was Wallenstein?

As happens in dreams, I stepped through the window insubstantial, soared like a bird over town and sleeping fields, like a raven on tireless wings. White lands spread beneath me, the dark curve of the Agara beckoning, a swift-flowing torrent too fast to be imprisoned in ice. A black tower glimmered with lights amid the whirling snow, the castle at Eger.

And yet something was wrong. The drawbridge was raised, the portcullis lowered. Lights glimmered in high windows but in the courtyard no one stirred.

Shots rang out, the stink of powder borne on the snow-laden wind. I circled, silent and helpless, listening to the cries of men. I watched. I saw the courtyard doors open, saw one man stagger out, a trail of blood in the snow behind him—Adam Trcka. I saw him make for the stables and I saw them shoot him down in cold blood, spilling across the dark stones like a sacrifice.

Helpless, I watched the muster in the courtyard, watched them kick him like a dog to be sure that he was dead. I watched them assemble, watched the drawbridge lowered, saw them march into the town. I was a dream, not even a ghost, not even a phantom. I followed through the silent streets to the mayor's house, the finest house in town, watched them kick down the door and pour inside. I saw. I saw all.

In Falkenau I sat bolt upright in the dark chamber, reaching for sword and pistol. Izabela came awake in one swift move as I stood up, flinging open the casement at the window as though I could fly in truth, as though my human eyes could bridge the distance I could in sleep. "What is the matter?" she said.

"Wallenstein is dead."

There was worry in her voice. "How do you know this?"

"I dreamed it," I said, my hands on the sill. Outside the snow still blew in swift gusts, but fresh or blown from tower roofs I could not tell. "I saw him start from his bed. I saw him run through with a halberd. No man survives that. He is dead." I closed my eyes as though that would block sight unphysical. "The Emperor has killed him."

Izabela put her hand on my shoulder and I flinched. I had not heard her leave the bed. "Do you dream things that are true?" she asked me quietly.

"Sometimes," I said. Whatever I might have feared in her knowing was eclipsed by the memory of Adam sprawled in the snow, his blood steaming.

She put her other hand against the front of my shirt, turning me from the window. "That must be useful."

"Not very," I said dryly. "What use to know when there is nothing I can do?"

She wet her lips like a cat, thinking. "There is much you can do," she said. "There is much you can do, knowing before you can know. Wallenstein's death changes everything."

"It means there will be no peace," I said.

"Does it?"

I opened my eyes. The wind was cold through the open window, snow swirling around us in the dark. Her pale skin glimmered as though she were made of moonlight. "It means the Emperor will not make peace with the Swedes," I said. She recalled me to myself, her hands warm through the linen of my shirt. I took a breath. I could think. Adam was only one man dead. There had been many such before.

"And then?"

"The Emperor has no general who is half so good," I said. "The rest of the lot are pigs. Tilly was good, but he's gone. The Swedes will roll over us."

"Then we change sides," Izabela said. I looked at her sharply and she smiled. "Why not join with the Protestant princes and be Sweden's ally? Take Falkenau back where she belongs, to the side her people love. You have said you care nothing for Pope or Emperor. Why serve them? Why play this game of thrones on a side you do not even believe in? If it is all one to you, then betray your master's murderer and preserve what is yours!"

I looked at her. "You'd like that, wouldn't you?"

"Wouldn't you?" Izabela asked. "What do you owe them? Your men fight for hire and they will just as readily fight for the Protestant princes as against them. An offensive in the spring against the Emperor's men unprepared and ill-commanded. . . . You are Graf Falkenau, and Wallenstein's man besides. You could have a strong voice in their counsels. The Protestant princes could bring the Emperor to bay, force a peace of their own forging. The only way we will have that is to make it so!"

I shook my head as though to clear it. "You will bewitch me into folly," I said.

"Is it folly?" Izabela demanded. "Do you not see the tactical situation before you? Half of Wallenstein's men will not follow the Emperor and the other half you have said are ill-commanded. It is winter. Everyone is bogged deep in snow. No one is moving. But at the thaw the Protestant princes can take Prague! Good God!" Izabela's hand tightened on my shirt. "Were I a man I could do it in three weeks with a thousand men! I could stuff a treaty down the Emperor's throat! Do not tell me that you cannot!"

I took a deep breath. "France is paying Emperor and King of Sweden both. Richelieu is playing both sides."

Izabela's face was serious as though she considered it, clockwork turning. "Until it becomes too expensive for him," she said. "You can make it too expensive. The Protestant princes can make it too expensive. Let us turn this war against him, that he may see the price of his own actions when the battle moves onto French soil instead of Bohemian. You can do this."

I nodded slowly. "I can write to others. We will not be told of Wallenstein's assassination for days yet, maybe weeks. The Emperor will not know we know. Not until it's too late." There had to be some use to this, to Adam dead, to the ruin of Bohemia. Some use, somehow. . . .

Izabela took both my hands in hers. "Change sides, Georg. Be my husband and my voice. Be my sword. Forge this peace."

I met her eyes. "Your husband in truth?"

Izabela swallowed. "Yes."

"I would not have that be a price," I said. "Your body for my allegiance." And yet I wanted her.

"Do not you see?" she said, and her voice broke. "It is the only way I can."

She stood there in the cold, her hair across her shoulders,

and I did see indeed. A bargain with an ally was not surrender. Izabela would never surrender.

It was not that a sword stood between me and Falkenau. It was that I must take that sword. No prince would command me, no God-sent queen justify my actions. The choice was mine, and thousands might live or die upon it, the course of history shifted in its bed though none should know my name, though none should remember Georg, Graf Falkenau.

I closed my eyes. No angels would come at my call. In this fallen world there would be no trumpets, no flash of light. There would be diplomacy and councils with men I did not like, and more than probably bloody battles in any event. But when I died it would not be for nothing. She would outlive me by decades, this glorious woman, Izabela and our children after. I should be a name in the lists of men who had died for this land, a man who had built a tiny corner, who had preserved an orchard or raised a tower, who had repaired a bridge or sired a daughter to stand on these walls in bright starlight to watch the stars or the courses of the wandering planets. Whether my bones lay in her crypts or on some distant field, I would have a place, Lord of Falkenau, now and ever.

"I will take your bargain," I said, and took Izabela's hands in mine. "And together we will weather every storm."

Her eyes glittered. "Like carrion birds," she said. "We stoop to conquer."

I kissed her there amid the falling snow that swirled about the towers of Falkenau.

DION EX MACHINA
4 BC

*D*ion *is one of my favorite characters in the Numinous World.*
Needless to say, Dion wanted a story of his own about his life
after Hand of Isis *and its tragic end. This story takes place many years*
later and is, oddly enough, inspired by a story I've never read. I've tried
to get my hands on Mary Renault's short story "According to Celsus" for
twenty years now, but I've never found it. Still, I like to think this story
is perhaps related, and that were she living she might like it.

It was Roman September, as the official news proclaimed
all over town, the September after the Grand Conjunction,
September when the terrible anniversaries of August were come
and gone. Twenty four years, Dion thought as he made his way
through the markets near the Canopic Gate in early morning,
the sun still slanting sideways over the walls of Alexandria.
The gates had been opened less than an hour, but the farmers
bringing in things from the countryside were already doing a
brisk business. He liked the mornings. Once he had seen them
from the other side, the end of a day that involved all night at the
Observatory, or in wine and conversation, or in love.

Twenty four years, my darling, Dion thought. And who
would have imagined it? Still here and still hale, and like to
be a great grandfather soon, the way that scamp Alexander is
going. There will be some girl's father calling on me, the way
he's seventeen going on thirty. He'll bring it to me, knowing
Demetria will be less sympathetic.

Dion strolled around a stall full of chickens clacking and clucking in their cages, raising a hand to forestall the seller. As though he looked like he was buying chickens! Surely his respectable dark robe over a finely worked chiton proclaimed him what he was, a scholar of discernment. He was not the sort of man to buy chickens!

In a quiet corner behind the stall, a young girl was standing with a baby on her shoulder, her wide dark eyes taking in all of the crowd, the horologers returning from the temple outside the gates with their gilded staffs and pleated linens, the busy drovers bringing in cattle from the countryside, the Roman guards on the gates standing at ease in their steel and scarlet, a doctor passing by in her litter with her white hair pinned severely close to her head, schoolboys rushing by yelling in the middle of some game, all the bustle and beauty of the City. The girl waited beside a tired donkey, its head down. On her shoulder, the baby craned to look, raising pudgy hands in delight at the spectacle. He, at least looked well fed, but his mother had a thin, pinched look, as though worry and travel and care had eaten from her.

For a moment he hesitated, but then he thought, do I look like a pimp or procurer? "Are you looking for someone, child?" he asked.

She looked at him uncomprehendingly and answered instead in Aramaic. "I'm sorry. I don't understand Greek."

Dion switched smoothly. "I asked if you were looking for someone, child. I am a Jew too, so we can speak Aramaic instead."

Relief flooded her eyes, and Dion thought she was very young, no more than fifteen or so. "Thank you, sir. My husband will be back soon, I'm sure. We've just gotten here, and we're looking for my cousin but I don't know where he lives and it seemed so much easier when we were coming to say we would find him in Alexandria but now the city is so big and we couldn't find anyone who looked like they spoke Aramaic . . ."

"You've come in through the wrong gate for that," Dion said. "The Jewish quarter is that way, but you'd find a kosher grocery or six in all the other markets, even the fish market. But this is the Canopic Market, and there's only one kosher grocer here. Not as many Jews live in this part of the city, you see."

"Do we have to stay in certain places?" There was a shadow of fear in her eyes, and he saw her hand tighten just a little on the baby's shawl.

"No," Dion said kindly. "Of course not. It's just that some neighborhoods are more Jewish than others. What does this cousin of yours do?"

"He's a cabinetmaker," she said. "Samuel the son of Reuben. He makes furniture. I thought that everyone would know him." She looked out over the square, where women and slaves alike were starting their shopping, the women calling to each other and greeting each other like long lost kin, when they'd probably seen each other the day before. "But now I see the city is too big. It's bigger even than Jerusalem."

"Alexandria is the largest city in the world," Dion said. "There are more than half a million people in the City proper. There are more Jews in Alexandria than Jerusalem, so you shan't lack for company." He smiled down at her. "I am Dion, and I am a scholar of astronomy, and a teacher at the Museum."

"Is that like a magi?" Something cautious lit in her eyes.

"Yes," Dion said. "You could call me a magus." He was rather surprised she should know what a magus was, country bred as she seemed to be.

"My name is Maryam," she said. "It's just that it's taken so long to get here, and my cousin's not really expecting us because there wasn't a way to send a letter. Everything is so much bigger and farther apart. We came by road from Pelusion, and we thought when we got to Pelusion from Gaza that we must be almost there, but then it's been another week and we were running short of everything . . ."

Dion blinked. "Why in the world didn't you sail? It's a much easier trip by sea, and cheaper really when you figure in the cost of travel." And easier on the baby too, Dion thought but did not say. The baby might be six months old, with his mother's wide dark eyes and sooty lashes. He was watching everything with fascination, pausing occasionally to throw out his arms and yell, "Ah ya ya ya!" If his mother had stinted herself in the journey, clearly she was still feeding him all right.

"We were afraid to," she said quietly. "King Herod's men guard the ports."

"Ah," Dion said as it all became clear. Since Herod was in his dotage, he'd gotten more than a little irrational. Living under a wretched old king was one thing, but one who had always had a bloody streak was just plain dangerous.

"Well, you are beyond Herod's reach now," Dion said proudly. "This is Alexandria, and it is still the freest city in the world. You can do anything or believe anything here. Well, anything as long as you pay your taxes to the man in Rome. I won't dignify that little pissant Octavian with the title of Caesar."

She looked confused.

"The Emperor Augustus," Dion said. "He used to be Octavian. He still is, as far as I'm concerned. Caesar's heir is dead these twenty four years."

Her voice was very low. "Aren't you afraid to say that?"

Dion laughed shortly. "My dear, this is Alexandria! If they

threw in jail everyone who cursed Octavian, the prison should be full to bursting! You can believe anything you want here, as long as you pay your taxes. Octavian doesn't care for our blessings, just our money." He glanced toward the Roman guards on the gate. One young man, in scarlet tunic under his leathers, had rather nice legs.

"Oh," she said, and there was a furrow between her brows that did not belong on the face of one so young.

"It's a safe place to be," Dion said kindly. "A good place to raise a child. You can start him in rhetoric and mathematics sooner than you think. Five or six is good. A clever boy can become anything here—teacher, sage, doctor, scientist, voyager."

"I had thought he would learn a trade," Maryam said, one hand caressing his unruly curls. "I hadn't asked yet or anything, but maybe he could learn cabinetry from my cousin. That's a good trade."

"It is," Dion said. The baby looked up at him, curious no doubt, his eye drawn by the bright borders on Dion's robe. "But a boy should have school too, even if he's to be a tradesman. You need to read and write to get by in Alexandria, read and write in Koine as well as Hebrew. And you've got to keep accounts. And a firm grounding in the sciences and literature even if you don't intend to go farther. Everyone ought to be familiar with schools of philosophy and understand how big the world is."

"I think he will understand that," she said, bending her face to plant a kiss on the top of his head.

"So let us wait for that husband of yours," Dion said. "Where did he go, anyway?"

"To see if he could find anyone who spoke Aramaic," she said.

"Well, you've found someone. We'll wait for him, and then

I will find you some breakfast and we'll start asking about this cousin of yours. There are some Jewish cabinetmakers in the Old Market. If he's not there, they probably know him."

"I couldn't possibly put you to all that trouble," she protested. "We're strangers to you, not even kin. And you must be an important man with business to attend to."

"I don't teach today until late afternoon," Dion said. "It would be my pleasure." Besides, he thought, looking at the baby, fresh from the country as they were they'd be an easy mark for anyone unscrupulous. He'd hate to see that. Though he thought the girl had a toughness underneath, a steel center she was only beginning to discover. He grinned at her. "Just call me Dion ex machina."

Maryam blinked. "I don't understand."

"It's a Latin joke," Dion said. "Never mind. When the gods throw something into one's path out of the blue."

"Oh." Her eyes widened, and she smiled, a beautiful smile that lit her entire face, naïve and wise at the same time. "Do you believe in angels then, who come to you in dreams?"

"Yes," said Dion gently, "I do."

COLD FRONTIER
505 AD

This short piece was written for my oldest friend, Robert Waters. Everyone has to tackle the story of King Arthur sooner or later, don't they? This is the story of Gull/Lydias/Charmian's life then.

My father held this land for Ambrosius, and held it well these twenty years, without strife or doubt. Yes, there was the scandal and the whispers when he married a witch, but my mother died long ago, proving that she was mortal after all, leaving nothing behind her except my gray eyes and a breath of the sea that swept through our rooms. My father, in his mourning, married no other and got no son, leaving no heir except me to a crumbling villa and a hill fort on a crag overlooking the sea, where we watched for Saxon raiders.

Three times they had come, and three times my father had pushed them back. So far we had been lucky. We had not seen more than one ship at a time, as many places had.

The villa had mosaiced floors, one with Perseus on winged Pegasus, holding Medusa's head before him, and a stone altar of Mithras inscribed on one side Valeria Victrix, and Sol Invictus on the other. It was for that he named me Valeria, seeking some tie to those men who were gone. Macsen took the legions over the sea long ago. We are not Roman now, except my father, who will never let Rome die in his heart. For him I must read Latin, and write in neat letters, copy every word in our few books, traveler's tales of places distant as the moon. And if there was any whisper of my mother in me, it did not make itself felt, save that sometimes the things that happened in books seemed more real to me than the world I stood in.

In the winter I could read. In the summer we labored and waited for the Saxons to make our toil in vain.

They rode in on a spring day, after Beltain but before Pentecost, eighty young men on scrubby horses, and the dust of their passage lingered in the air.

"The Saxons will come to Caer Leon," their leader said, "And we will be here before them. When they beach their ships we will be waiting with horse and steel, and we will drive them back into the sea." He had an old helm made pretty with a white plume, and I could not see his face.

Behind him, his second rode bareheaded and unshaven, his long red hair caught behind him in a long tail, the same bay as his horse. He winked at me, and I turned my head, but not before I saw him smile.

"This is Bedwyr son of Griffith," their leader said. He dismounted and saluted my father like a Centurion to a Senator. He was dark and small and with his helmet off was hardly taller than I. "I am Artorius, the nephew of Ambrosius. These are my Companions."

"Of course they are," I said. "I know my Arrian too."

SMALL VICTORIES
1800—1810 AD

*A*nother story with Dion, almost two thousand years later. Dion is a small girl, but still absolutely Dion. And then there is Emrys . . . . We will see more of these versions of them in my upcoming novel Fortune's Wheel.

Her name was Victory, and she had never known anything but war. She was a child of the Revolution, born the month that Robespierre was guillotined, and the war had lasted forever.

When she was small they had lived in a little house in Marseilles. It was on a narrow street, and from the windows of the third floor room where she slept with her older brother and sister you could see the masts of the ships in the harbor moving over the roofs, see the sails catching the wind as they moved out to sea. Her stepmother had always been afraid of a knock on the door. If someone came she would catch at her throat before she went to answer it.

"She is afraid," Victory's older brother told her, "that someone has denounced Papa."

She almost didn't remember the little house. They had moved to a bigger one, on a street where you couldn't hear the sea. It had carpet on the stairs, and her baby brother was born there.

Now they lived in a much bigger house, with a park around it and a fountain and lots of grass to play on. There were ten servants and lots of rooms, and her older brother had a pony.

Papa was still gone. Now they said that he was a hero. For a while everyone said he was going to die, and her stepmother had black dresses made up so that when he did she would have something to wear.

But then he didn't die and he came home.

He looked very thin, and his black hair was streaked with gray at the temples, and he was very glad to see them all. Victory was glad too, even though she was one of the girls in the middle, she and her sister, and not the baby who was cute or her older brother who could ride a horse.

It was summer, and he hadn't been home long when they had a party.

There were big tables set up on the lawn and games for people to play with tenpins. There were some men who played violins and a tent if it was too sunny. Her stepmother rented six peacocks to walk around showing off their feathers.

Papa thought that was funny. "They just shit everywhere," he said. "Why do we want that?" But her stepmother thought they were very aristocratic.

The party was fun. It went on all day, and there were lots of people who came and went. Some of them had children too, though most of them were older. And some of the ladies wanted to pinch her cheeks and say how cute she was, just like a little Catalan shepherdess in her white lawn dress and her bare feet.

Her stepmother flushed at that and told her sharply to go find her shoes, what was she, a ragamuffin?

Victory decided that it would be better to stay out of sight for a while, since she'd lost her shoes and didn't know where they were. Nurse would probably find them eventually. But it might be better not to attract attention until she did.

She climbed up one of the trees and stayed there, lying on her stomach on a big branch, nibbling on a piece of bread, watching the people down the hill at the party walking around and eating and talking to each other. Two of the peacocks were fighting and the footmen were trying to separate them. She thought the ladies looked like peacocks too. She wondered if they'd have a fight and throw their big hats at each other. Or maybe there would be a duel. That might be interesting.

Someone was coming across the lawn semi-furtively, looking back as though he didn't want to be seen. It was a young man with long black hair pulled back in a tail, a dark blue coat and buff pants, with a black sling holding his left arm. He stopped under the tree and sat down with his back against it.

Victory leaned down to see what he was up to.

Stealthily, he pulled a book out of his pocket and opened it, settling back against the tree trunk.

Victory threw a chunk of bread at him. It bounced off his head and landed on the book.

He looked up. "Strange birds in this tree," he said, smiling.

"Tweet," said Victory.

"What are you doing up there?" he asked.

She shrugged. "Nothing. What are you reading?"

He closed the book with one hand. The other was still in the sling. "*In the Year 2440*. It's about a man who travels 600 years in to the future and what he finds there."

"Is it yours?" she asked, sitting up on the branch.

"It belongs to your father," he said. "I didn't think he'd mind if I borrowed it for a few minutes. I've read it before, and I wanted to come back to it like an old friend."

"What happened to your book?" she asked.

"I lost it somewhere or other," he said. "You could come down out of the tree."

Victory considered and then climbed down. "What happened to your arm?" she asked, sitting down on the grass.

"I was shot."

She thought he had a very nice face, even though his legs were sort of too long for the rest of him. "Did it hurt?"

"It hurt awfully at first," he said. "But it doesn't hurt anymore. When you're a soldier you have to get used to things like that."

"Are you a soldier?"

"I'm a captain," he said. "In the Hussars. But I'm detached right now."

"What's your name?"

"Is this a parlor game? Honoré-Charles Reille. And yours?"

"Victory," she said. "Have you had lots of adventures?"

"Some." He put the book down on the grass and stretched his legs out in the shade, leaning back against the tree. "I got to carry a secret message into a besieged city. That was an adventure."

"Tell me about it," she said. "That sounds fun."

He put his hat on the grass and ran his hands through his hair. "General Bonaparte knew that your father was holding the city of Genoa. You've heard about that?"

She nodded.

"And so he decided to bring lots of troops and beat the Austrians while they were all camped around Genoa watching your father and not watching their backs. But he knew that there was no way that your father could know what he was up to, and that help was on the way. So he ordered me to sneak into Genoa and tell him."

Victory sat up very straight. "How did you do that?"

"I snuck past the British fleet at night on a smuggling boat. It was painted black and it was hard to see against the water. The smugglers got me in as close as they could, and then I took off my coat and my hat and my sword, and climbed overboard into the black water." He paused for a breath, and grinned at her. "I'm a good swimmer because I grew up swimming all the time at home, so I swam very quietly past the British ships and they never saw me. When I got to shore, I went to your father and told him the secret message. That he was supposed to hold until 12 Prairial, and then after that he could make terms with the Austrians, but that he had to hold them there until 12 Prairial."

Victory hugged her knees up to her chin. "What happened then?"

"Then I was inside the besieged city with your father. And it was a long fight. We didn't have much to eat, and the Austrians kept attacking. And we kept pushing them back. 12 Prairial came, and we didn't have any more news. So your father said we'd just keep holding as long as we could. I got shot on 14 Prairial, and on 15 Prairial he finally asked the Austrians for terms. In the meantime, General Bonaparte trapped the Austrians and beat them."

"That's so . . ." Victory couldn't think of enough words to describe it. "Terrific," she said.

"It pretty much was," he said.

She laughed. "I think you ought to marry a princess for that," she said. "Just like in the stories."

"I'm not sure a princess would want to marry me," he said, smiling back. "I'm a merchant's son. And besides, we don't have any princesses anymore."

"Then will you marry me?"

He didn't laugh at her. Victory was glad of that. He looked at her, as though seriously considering. "How old are you?"

"Almost six," she said. "I was born in Thermidor."

"I think six is a little young to get married," he said. "You probably need to wait a few years."

"How old are you?"

"Almost twenty-four," he said. "I was born in Thermidor too."

"You're not too old for me," she said. "Not if you wait."

He did laugh then, and she thought it was a very nice laugh. "You'll have forgotten all about me by then. Come on, little Victory. The people are starting to go into dinner, and your nurse will be looking for you."

He helped her up. Or maybe she helped him up. After all, he had a bad arm. They went up the lawn to the party, Victory skipping a little to avoid the peacock shit. He stepped in it, but he didn't notice and she didn't tell him.

Her father came down and swooped her up. "Where are your shoes?" he asked.

"I don't know." Victory shrugged. When she looked around the young man was gone. "Where did he go?" she asked.

"Where's your nurse?" her father said. "You need some dinner too. And then it's your bedtime. And how do you get such snarls in your hair?" He started trying to work a tangle out of her long dark curls.

"I don't know," Victory said. She looked after the young officer, but she didn't see him anywhere. "I'm going to marry him," she said.

It was ten years before she saw him again.

The ballroom of the Tuileries was hot and stuffy, even this early in the evening. The candles and the press of bodies made that inevitable. Victory carefully lifted her skirts as she climbed the stairs, trying not to trip. She had told her stepmother it was too long at the dressmaker's, but she'd insisted it was fine. Now Victory would spend all night trying not to fall on her face. If she ever got a dance, which wasn't terribly likely. This was only the second time she'd attended an Imperial ball, and the first time she hadn't danced at all, only stood around with Marianne, looking more and more stupid as the evening went on.

Victory knew she wasn't pretty. Golden girls with pink and white complexions were pretty, girls with large breasts and curving shoulders and décolletage that invited a second look. She was short and sallow, at barely sixteen still boyish and too thin, with lank brown hair that wouldn't take a curl no matter how much time she spent on it. She could singe her hair off with irons and it still wouldn't curl. The only feature she liked were her eyes, dark and smoky brown, fringed with long lashes, deep and (she hoped) mysterious. Unfortunately, anyone would have trouble seeing them, as the curls had already fallen out of her bangs and lay in a sodden mass across her forehead that she had to peep out under.

They were announced at the top of the stairs. Fortunately, no one would see her anyway, behind her father and stepmother and her older sister. At the bottom of the stairs her sister was claimed by her fiancé, and her stepmother was already making a beeline for Madame la Marechale Lannes, who had recently come out of mourning and could always be counted on to know everything.

Her father turned to her, one eyebrow raised.

"Don't you dare," Victory whispered urgently.

"All right then," he said, and gave her a wink as he headed off to join Marechal Berthier, who no doubt had something stronger than punch to drink.

There could be no fate worse than to be the kind of girl who doesn't get anyone to dance with her but her own father! It was better to sit it out, fanning oneself, looking like the kind of girl who was too exhausted from all her previous dances to dance this one.

Marianne was standing in the corner behind the punchbowl, an enormous painted fan held right up to her nose. Victory sidled over and joined her. "What's the matter with you?" she whispered. "That fan's eating you!"

Marianne dipped it momentarily, long enough for Victory to see the enormous spot on her chin, rendered more conspicuous by a vast quantity of powder and some sort of creamy concealer meant for someone with much darker skin.

"Oh no!" she whispered sympathetically.

"I wanted to stay home," Marianne replied, "But my father said I shouldn't act like a little fool, so here I am!"

"I'm so sorry!"

"If I just keep the fan here, maybe nobody will notice," Marianne said miserably.

Victory nodded, and refrained from saying; nobody will notice the huge spot on your chin because they'll be wondering why that crazy girl's hiding behind a fan. "I'll stand with you," Victory said. "Nobody's going to dance with me anyway, and we can look like sophisticated women who have much more interesting things to talk about than dancing."

Across the room, the pack of unmarried men were clustered around the buffet table instead of the punch bowl, their brilliant uniforms glittering with gold braid. A few pairs of tall boots gleamed.

"Aren't they supposed to be wearing evening shoes?" Victory said. Her father certainly was.

Marianne nodded. "Of course they are. But they wear boots

to show they're cavalry. It's so much more romantic."

"Oh." Victory cocked her head at the gorgeous pelisses, the pants so tight they looked as though they might split, the velvet and gold lace. "We'd know that anyhow."

There was a burst of laughter from the group, and a smaller man stowed what looked like a flask in his breast pocket. "Onward, men!" he laughed. "If I dance with a debutante, we all have to!"

"Onward!" another agreed, and the whole pack of them came across the room, sizing girls up like so many horses on a picket line.

"Oh God!" Marianne moaned.

The man who had spoken stopped in front of her. "If I might have the honor, mademoiselle?"

Marianne cast a desperate look at Victory, and put her un-fanned hand in his. "Yes."

He blanched when he saw her chin and tried not to laugh. Which made Victory mad. She stood along the wall seething.

"If you would, mademoiselle?" A hand in an immaculate white glove had appeared in front of her.

She turned about and saw what was attached to it, an apparently infinite stretch of scarlet wool trimmed with gold braid, dolman laced across his chest, a scarlet pelisse thrown over his shoulder trimmed in fur, and above that, a very long way up, a pleasant enough face with olive skin and dark eyes. She looked down, which was a mistake, as his white pants were incredibly tight and outlined all of his masculine attributes to perfection.

He offered his hand again. "Mademoiselle?"

"Oh, yes," she said belatedly and let him pull her onto the dance floor.

They rounded the first turn without disaster. He mumbled something.

"What?" she shrieked as they went round again.

He looked at her and she thought there was something vaguely familiar about his face, as though they'd met before. "I said, it's unseasonably warm, don't you think?"

"Yes," Victory said.

Which carried them through the turn.

She should have begged off, said she had a headache or something. She should have known better. Now he would think she had fluff between her ears. Which was not at all the problem. In fact, it would be something of the solution. At school until last month, it had not been the problem at all. Even the headmistress, Madame Campan, who thought that girls should have an education, had been fairly appalled by Victory.

"The applications of higher mathematics in Kepler's *Laws of Planetary Motion* are not a suitable subject of study for young ladies," she had said, "You are a debutante, not a scientist."

"Kepler's *Laws of Planetary Motion*," she said.

Her escort blinked. "What about them?"

Victory shrugged. "Do you like them?"

He laughed, and the smile transformed his face from pleasant to really handsome. "I like them well enough. I don't think I can name them anymore. It's been a long time since I was in school." He nodded to the glitter of decorations on his chest, all the jewelry of an Imperial Aide de Camp. "I ran away from school to join the Army of the Republic a long time ago."

Victory put her head to the side. "Why?"

He blinked again, looking almost shy. "Do you really want to know?"

"Yes."

"So I wouldn't have to take a Latin exam," he said. "I knew I was going to do very badly and they'd write to my father, and

I thought, if I just run away and join the army, I won't have to take it!"

Victory laughed and pushed her bangs back with her free hand. "That's a good story. Were you good in school?"

He shrugged. "Not bad."

"Kepler or Copernicus?"

"Copernicus," he said. "The rings of Saturn are more fun."

"Goethe or Schiller?"

"Oh, Goethe of course," he said. "Doesn't everybody write poems about dying for love when they're seventeen?"

"Arthur or Charlemagne?"

"Arthur," he said decisively. "But not Lancelot."

"He's a later addition anyway," Victory said. "*In The Year 2440* or *Dangerous Liaisons?*"

"Impossible." He shook his head. "Time travel or pornography? I can't make the choice."

"How about time travel with pornography?" Victory suggested. "Someone could write it."

"Someone could."

"Egypt or Rome?"

"Rome," he said, coming out of the last turn as the song ended. "I've never been to Egypt."

"You weren't on the Egyptian campaign then?"

They stood by the edge of the floor.

He shook his head. "I wasn't with Bonaparte's corps then. I wasn't with him in Italy either. I was in Genoa with Massena."

"Oh!" she said, and with a rush it came back to her—the summer day after Genoa, and the young officer under a tree reading her father's book, the one she had wanted to wait for her. She felt the blood rush to her face. But how would he know? She had been not quite six. The years between six and sixteen are nearly forever. Surely he wouldn't recognize her.

People were walking around them. He put his head to the side, a curiously intent expression on his face. "May I ask your name, Mademoiselle?"

"Victory," she said.

"That's all?"

She gave him a quick glance upward. "That's all."

"No last name?"

She grinned. "Do you think you've earned my last name?"

"What do I need to do to earn your last name?"

"You'll think of it," she said, and slipped between people, making her escape. She looked back over her shoulder, but he had not moved, still staring after her.

She regained Marianne at the wall behind the punchbowl. Marianne was fanning herself feverishly. "Oh my God."

"What?"

"I just made a total fool of myself. That man there? I asked him to marry me when I was six." Victory stuck her head behind her own fan.

Marianne looked toward the dance floor. "Well, it's been a long time," she said practically. "He probably doesn't remember."

"You don't think he will?"

"Probably not."

"I think his name is Honoré-Charles," she said, wracking her brain. "I think so."

Marianne nodded emphatically. "Oh yes. My mother made me memorize them all. General Honoré-Charles Reille, Aide de Camp to the Emperor himself. He's thirty four and a bachelor. He's not a baron yet, but I imagine it's only a matter of time before he's ennobled."

"Oh dear Lord," Victory said. "Jesus Christ on toast with

bacon. I can't believe I made such a fool of myself."

"It was only a dance," Marianne said. "He's probably forgotten about you already."

Victory looked out from behind her fan.

He was easy to find, even in the crowd. Now he was standing by the buffet table with the small man who had danced with Marianne. They had been joined by an enormous man with sideburns and a long moustache, who had a silver flask quite openly in his hand. He offered it to Honoré, who drank and then passed it to the fourth member of their party. She took it, laughing, and Victory's stomach clinched. Her blonde hair was piled on top of her head and fell in charming ringlets, and her red velvet and brocade dress showed every curve. She must be thirty or so, but she put her hand on the small man's arm with graceful familiarity, tilting the flask back and drinking before she gave it back to its owner. He laughed, and said something that amused everyone in the group.

"Who are the others?" she hissed at Marianne.

"Let's see." Marianne flipped her fan and gazed over the top. "The man I was dancing with is Colonel Jean-Baptiste Corbineau. He's the younger brother of General Corbineau who was killed at Eylau. He's a bachelor too. The big man is General Baron Gervais Subervie. Married. Very married."

Victory looked at them again. Subervie had said something funny, and Honoré threw his arm about his shoulders, adding another line to the joke. The woman tossed her head, laughing, and not a single curl fell down.

"Who's the woman?"

Marianne dropped her voice. "We're not supposed to notice her! She's a courtesan!"

"Ohhhhhh."

"Her name is Ida St. Elme, and she used to go with General Moreau, and then she went with Marechal Ney. She wouldn't be here at all if she weren't an old friend of Josephine's, from back in the Directory."

"Then why is she still here?" Victory asked. "The Empress is out."

Marianne shrugged. "It's very strange. I wonder who she sleeps with now."

"So do I," Victory said grimly. It must be nice to just stand and talk with those men, without wondering if one were a fool. He would have completely forgotten about her. Of course he would, with beautiful blonde courtesans hanging on his arm.

The blonde glanced in her direction, then put her hand on Honoré's, leaning toward him to say something in a low voice.

Victory tossed her head to make it clear she could care less. "Kepler's *Laws of Planetary Motion*," she muttered.

The gavotte was ending. Honoré broke away from the group, the blonde looking after him encouragingly, and made his way around the room. He was not coming toward her. He wasn't. He was just coming to get punch. Or something. He probably wanted punch. He probably loved punch.

He stopped right in front of her as the first strains of the waltz began. "Mademoiselle? May I have the pleasure?"

"Yes," said Victory with a brilliant smile.

HOW THE LADY OF CATS
CAME TO NAGADA
8000 BC

This story comes from the first days of the world, when there were no great cities and in the Black Land the building of the pyramids was more than four thousand years in the future.

Once, long ago in the dawn of the world, when all the cities that are were no more than collections of a few houses of mud brick, there was a bride named Meri. She and her husband lived in one room on the edge of the desert, in the smallest house in the village. He was an orphan, and no one lived there but them.

Sometimes Meri found it very lonely, used as she was to the house by the riverbank where she had grown up, with her grandmother and her father and her four tall brothers and their wives and children. She missed the laughing and singing, and the babies playing underfoot on the floor while she made baskets. But her husband, Neshi, had always been alone, and she loved him.

Besides, it was not as though she could not go home. It was less than a morning's walk to her father's house, and she was always welcome. Her nieces would come running when they saw her, shouting about all the things they had been doing and telling her all of their secrets—where a goose had laid her eggs in the reeds along the river, and where the herons were fishing.

From Meri's house they could see the river, but even at the height of the floods they barely topped the small square fields that belonged to Neshi. If the flood wasn't very high their fields would not be touched at all.

That was what had happened this year. The flood had been bad, so bad that even her father, who owned a piece of bottomland, had shaken his head and muttered prayers. Further up, where they lived, the flood had not come at all. The fields that should have been deep in life-giving water baked in the sun.

And so they had carried water in jars, backbreaking work in the summer heat, she and Neshi. They had planted only one field, and watered it twice a day by hand, making the trip down to the river over and over again, pouring the water out on the soil and watching in run into cracks that should not be there.

There were sprouts. There were some that grew, no matter how poor the soil. There were some that grew even with nothing to nourish them but the water from the bucket. Some sprouts survived. There would be some wheat, too little, but some.

By the river, her father had melons, and if every few days someone came by on chance, bringing a few vegetables, it was not charity. One of her brothers just happened to be passing by and thought he'd bring a few cucumbers.

When the wheat was reaped and stored in the shed, Meri looked at it with dismay. There was so little, and much must be left for seed in a few months. It would do no good if the flood rose and they had no seed. There was very little left for making bread, and none to trade.

Neshi knew it, and she saw the defeated slump of his shoulders. They had said he was not good enough for her, and he knew it was true. He could not keep a bride without starving her, or relying on her family's charity.

It was three months yet until the river rose.

The sun baked all the land, Black Land and Red Land alike, and they were not the only ones hungry. At night Meri or Neshi would get up and go in the storehouse with a club, laying about to startle the mice and small creatures that would come in to steal the grain. Meri hated killing them, but Neshi would flail about with a fury, the only thing in his world he could fight. For how could a man fight the river that did not rise or the grain that did not grow?

Every night they would trade, getting up and going in the dark.

That was how Meri first saw her. Coming out into the clear, cool night air, she took a deep breath. The moon was already beginning to set.

A shadow streaked across the yard, a lean striped wildcat, something struggling in her mouth. She paused at the edge of the field, and Meri got a good look at her. She was gray and tan, the better to melt into the rocks where she usually hunted, in the steep hills of the Red Land. But hunger had driven her to the river too. She must hunt. And the granaries and storehouses of the Black Land attracted the small animals she lived on. A rat was struggling in her mouth even now. She turned and looked at Meri, and Meri looked back.

"Take your fill, Sister," Meri said. "Any rat you take is one less to eat what we have struggled for."

The cat waited a moment, and then turned and disappeared into the darkness.

After that, Meri saw her many times. She slunk around the edges of the farm, hunted the shed and the field at night. Once or twice Meri saw her take down prey, and more than that she found a few shreds of bone and skin that had been one of the small animals that took the grain. Meri began to watch for her. She thought perhaps she was getting fatter. That was satisfying. It meant that there were many fewer mice.

It was true that there were. No longer did they wake to droppings everywhere, to chewed baskets leaking seed where the rats had been. At night when they went in the storehouse, no longer was it absolutely crawling with mice who scattered at the light of the torch. The little animals could hear her and Neshi coming, but they feared far more the silent stalker.

One evening Meri went out to check and opened the storehouse door. To her surprise, Sister was there and did not leap or hide at her approach. Instead, she lay on her side panting.

Meri stopped in her tracks.

The wildcat regarded her, but didn't get up from where she lay on a piece of sacking. Her green eyes were wide.

"Oh . . ." Meri breathed, for she saw why in a second. Protruding from the wildcat's vagina was the back end and tail of a tiny kitten, her muscles working to push it out. "Oh," she said, and slowly crouched down. "I am sorry, Sister. I did not mean to disturb you at your birthing."

She watched while the wildcat pushed it out, and turned about to get at it, licking its tiny face and pink nose, shoving it against her furry side.

The door opened. "Meri?" Neshi said.

The wildcat sprung to her feet hissing, and Neshi raised his club.

"No, wait!" Meri jumped up, grabbing the club from his hand. "That's Sister. She's the one who's been eating the mice and rats, like I said. Leave her alone! She's having her kittens in here."

"In here?" Neshi said dubiously. "I never heard of a wildcat having her kittens in a storehouse."

"Why not?" Meri said. "If she's in here all the time with a litter of kittens, there won't be a mouse or rat anywhere around. The only thing better than having her hunt in here would be having a bunch of cats in here all the time. And a mother who's feeding kittens is going to be eating a lot."

Neshi scratched his head. "I suppose," he said. "I mean, it's not like she eats grain."

"She doesn't touch the grain," Meri said. "Just the rats." She put her arms around his neck. "Come now. Let her stay."

She saw his eyes warm as they did when she touched him, when he forgot for a moment how bad everything was. "If you want me to," he said.

Meri nodded. "Go on. I'll stay here a while until she settles down again."

Neshi went out, and Meri sat down against the door. The cat's eyes were on her, and Meri saw the ripples moving along her side. This kitten was not the only one.

"It's all right, Sister," she said softly. "You are safe. Nothing will bother you here, with me and Neshi watching over you."

The kitten mewed, rooting at the sacking, and the wildcat walked around it twice before she lay down. It burrowed into her and she purred while the next contraction rippled across her brindled fur.

Meri leaned back. She must have dozed, for she dreamed that there were three kittens, gray and tan, with pink ears turned back and little flailing claws. She reached for one, and then looked up.

Their mother was enormous, bigger than a house, a great gray cat sitting on her haunches, and her green eyes glowed in the darkness. Meri was as small as a mouse between her paws.

"Do not fear, Little Sister," the cat said. "You have done a kindness to Me, and in the process have done yourself much good as well. We can help one another, your people and mine. Your grain is safe, and your seeds for the next season as well. You will have enough to plant, because my Daughter and her children will guard it for you, while you give them room to grow and a safe place from the desert vultures. And in time they will come when you call, and let you touch them and hold them, for they will never remember a time when you were not their foster mother. Cats will walk with you all your life, for you are blessed by the Lady of Cats. And when eight times the moon has waxed and waned, you will bear your child in safety and need fear no scorpions in the cradle, for Sister will kill any that are in your house."

Meri bent her head, for she knew she spoke to a goddess. "Gracious Lady, I ask no blessings for me, though I am thankful for your kindness. But the Black Land is parching beneath the sun, and if the river does not rise I do not know what we will do! I do not know what will happen to Neshi and all my family if there is no flood this year. Can you make the river to rise?"

It seemed to her that the great cat purred. "Little Sister," she said, "There is nothing I need to do. Far away, many days and nights journey to the south, the rain is falling. The rain is falling in great sheets, drenching the jungles and overflowing the lakes, rushing in great torrents over the falls. And it is there that the river is born. In a month the flood will rise, and your fields will be covered in life-giving water. You do not need to ask it as a blessing, for it will already happen."

Meri awoke in the clear hour before dawn. Three brindled kittens nursed and wiggled beside their mother. Meri stood up and stretched her cramped body. The wildcat watched her warily, but did not move.

Eight moons. It was possible. When the grain stood green in the fields waiting for the harvest she might hold her own child in her arms. And she would fear no scorpions or rats, for Sister would not let any such live. By then she would be teaching her kittens to hunt in the tall wheat.

"Blessings on you, Sister," Meri said. And she went to get a bowl of water. Surely giving birth was thirsty work.

PRINCE OVER THE WATER
1040 AD

The Lady of the Dead has many names in many languages, but there is no place where Her wishes may be disregarded, least of all by a witch who owes her homage. Here, in a distant land at the end of the world, Gull is still bound by old oaths and still fears nothing while under her Lady's protection. In Her service another quest begins.

The dream came to me on the eve of Samhuinn, when true dreams come. "Stand up," she said, "And come with me." And so I stood and walked with her.

It seemed to me in sleep that I was far from the smell of peat fires and sheep dung, far from the fresh scent of evergreens that grew on the headland, far from the scent of the sea. I followed her in sleep through a room paved with stars, where cold did not reach and the sighing of the waves did not follow.

"Come with me," she said, and a vast shape of wings stretched around her, black as starless night, black as deep caves. Her eyes were gray, and looking in them was like looking into the heart of the clouds.

"I will obey you, Lady," I said, for I knew who she was then, the Storm Queen who we do not name, she who rides upon the wind to take the brave men home, avenger and Lady of the Dead.

It seemed we stood in some vast place, in some echoing chamber where high above light fell from holes in the ceiling. The air was close and warm, and all along the walls were rolls of paper, stacked and covered neatly, tagged with long strips of paper and pieces of dyed cloth.

I started. On the floor beside the door a snake curled, waiting.

"Snakes are not death in dreams," she said, and she sounded amused.

"I'm sorry, Lady," I said, but I gave the snake a wide berth. It frightened me as much as the rest of this place fascinated me.

"Mac Bethad has killed the King," she said. "Donnchad is murdered at Dunsinane, and his blood cries out for vengeance. By the oaths you swore him, and your father before you, you must be an instrument to my hand."

"My Lady," I said, choosing my words carefully, "It is true that my father swore a mighty oath to Donnchad. If Donnchad were besieged, or if he faced battle with an army of his foes, I have no doubt that my father should lead all his men to his aid, in accordance with his word. But when the news came to us that Donnchad was slain soon after Lammas, and all his kin with him, the deed was already done. Mac Bethad sits upon the throne of Scotland. And though we might wreak vengeance upon him, no good can come of it to the living."

"No good indeed," she said, and her voice wakened shadows. Out of the shade of one of the great pillars a boy and girl came forth, talking to each other and playing in some language I did not understand, playing as though they did not see us. They were alike as twin lambs, with long dark hair and dark eyes, seven years old, clad together in tunics of white cloth. My heart leaped, and I felt tears start in my eyes, though I did not know why.

"By sun and moon," she said. "Your promise binds you."

The boy looked up and he saw me, smiled as though I were some beloved nurse he recognized, started toward me with his arms outstretched.

"Murdered," she said, and her voice rang like lightning in the clouds. "While you slept beside the river in the land of the dead. You were vowed to protect him, and you have not been released. Now he calls to you."

The room spun around me, and it seemed instead that we were outdoors on some great moor. I could smell the frost in the air, see the stars of winter wheeling above me. Horsemen galloped toward us, and I saw the bundle across one of their saddles. He had fair hair and light eyes, but he was the same boy, his hands bound together and his face streaked with dirt, younger than before, perhaps five instead of seven. His frightened eyes met mine. "Help me," he whispered. "Please."

I tried to grab for the reins, but my hands were insubstantial as mist.

The horsemen swept past, riding hard, their horses' breaths steam in the still night.

I closed my eyes. "Who is he?" I whispered.

"Mael, the only son of Donnchad. He lives still, carried away by Mac Bethad's men to a life of thralldom in some foreign city."

I opened my eyes. In her dark cloak, she looked less like the Lady of Storms and more like some woman I might know, with her heart shaped face and raven hair, scars upon her white arms. "What must I do?" I asked.

"Find him," she whispered, and I awoke.

It was dawn on the day of Samhuinn, and I lay in my bed. Beside me, my daughter Moirin slept peacefully. I could hear the sound of her breath, and her gold hair spread across the pillow, escaped from braids in sleep. She was ten years old. Her brother had already left to sleep with the fosterlings, since he was made a page to Crinain last spring. Carefully, so as not to wake her, I got up.

It only took a moment to pull on thick stockings, and to get my heavy wool dress on over my tunic. I found my boots beneath the bed and tugged them on, and took my cloak from beside the door.

Above, the watch was changing. Men were stomping toward the kitchens, rubbing their hands together, eager for porridge and whiskey. The night had been long, but we dare not cease watching, even on a holy night, not since the days of Somerled. I knew I should find my brother above.

Erik Thorfinnson stood on the battlements, looking out at the mist rising over Scapa Flow. He stood half a head taller than I, and I was by no means a small woman, with our father's bulk and broad shoulders. Erik and I did not favor him in other ways. We looked like our mother, Einiad, who had been a chief's daughter in Iceland, blond and fair, with eyes like ice or the pale sky after a storm at sea. I came and stood beside him, my hands next to his on the stone.

"I have dreamed, brother," I said.

He looked at me sideways, his mouth quirking a little. "Should that surprise me, sister? Many times you have dreamed, and dreamed true. Did you not tell me of the sinking of the Swan of Norway before it happened? Or that our father should return safe from battle when you were no more than a child yourself? What did you dream, Ilona?"

"Things I did not entirely understand," I said, and it seemed to me in the pure clear daylight with the sea breeze pulling at my hair that some of it was already indistinct. There had been a strange room, and warm sunshine coming in from above, a snake and boy and girl twins . . . "The son of Donnchad lives,"

I said. "He is carried away in to slavery by Mac Bethad's men, who do not dare to kill him."

My brother took a long, deep breath. He let it out again. He did not ask me if I were certain. We had no need of such questions. We were the children of Thorfinn alike. "Where is he taken?"

"I don't know," I said. So little to go on. A moor, and the smell of bracken. It could be anywhere, anywhere across the highlands. No, not just anywhere. There was no scent of the sea, no sound of running water. And I did not see the familiar shapes of mountains against the sky. Somewhere I had not been, which narrowed it down a bit. In my marriage I had gone far south, and once to the land of Northumbria. It was not some place I knew.

"Away," I said. "But he lives. And they will want him far from home, where any ploughman might recognize him, or take his child's words for something. Far away, no one will believe a little boy who claims to be a prince." I touched my brother's arm. There was something I didn't quite remember, some long ago fear of chains and a procession through a great city. They would not kill him, yet. "Erik, he still lives."

"And where there is life there is hope?" He gave me a sideways glance again. Warrior he might be, but he should call it cowardice to kill a child of five, no matter whose get he was. Erik followed the old ways in his heart, though he wore the cross on his breast as a matter of fact. One can't be too careful in devotions to the gods, or leave out any whose offense might matter. Besides, Erik had said often enough that some of the angels were doughty fellows.

"Our father has an oath."

Erik turned and took me by the shoulders. "Is it our father's oath that moves you, Ilona? Or something else?"

I shifted uncomfortably under his gaze. "I saw her, the Storm

Queen. She said I must, or be foresworn of some promise I made ere I was born. That I must obey, and be an instrument in her hand."

His blue eyes searched my face. Then he turned away. I saw that his hands clenched and unclenched on the battlement. "That is a mighty burden, sister."

I put my hand on his shoulder. I was the elder by fifteen months, but we had always breathed with one breath, as though we had never been parted, even though the years had carried him over land and sea while I was married far in the south. "Erik, I cannot disobey." I searched for the words. "And he is a child. You are the father of young sons yourself."

"He is not our kin," Erik said.

I said nothing and waited.

At last Erik let out a great sigh. "Where will you go?" he asked.

I had not thought I knew until this moment. "Dunsinane," I said. "That is where Donnchad was murdered, and where the trail begins."

"And where Mac Bethad now sits as King of Scotland."

"That too," I said, and smiled. "But if I do the Storm Queen's work, I shall expect her aid. And I am not without resources of my own."

"They say Mac Bethad's queen is a black witch," Erik said.

"I shall not fear that," I said primly. "Let it not be said that Ilona Thorfinn's daughter fears any other witch."

"Well then," Erik said, and he laughed. "Let it not be said indeed. The Seven Stars stands at anchor in Scapa Flow. I suppose I will bear you to Scotland, my sister."

HORUS INDWELLING
285 ℬℭ

*L*ydias *of Miletus, the main character of my novel* Stealing Fire, *is one of my favorite characters in the Numinous World. The end of the book leaves him beginning his life again, barely thirty years old, with the campaigns of Alexander behind him and the rest of his life before him. I think there are several more stories about Lydias and his adventures that come before this one, when Alexander's body at last comes to the city he founded.*

While we have no accounts of Alexander's actual funeral in Alexandria, it probably occurred at about this time. The procession, however, is not made up. It comes from an account of the Ptolemaia eight years later, over the top as it is! Nobody did over the top like the Ptolemies!

The stars paled over Alexandria in anticipation of the glowing orb of the sun. Already some noise filtered over the garden wall, people in the streets getting an early start to this day of days. I stole a piece of bread from the kitchen as though I were no more than a boy again and went to eat it on the bench beneath the young peach tree, its branches in bud but not yet blooming, away from the bustle in the house.

Demetria found me there. "Hello father," she said, plopping down on the bench beside me. "I thought I'd find you out here." She was already dressed, her white chiton spotless and her hair pinned up at the back of her neck in a dozen bronze pins which it was already escaping from. There were no pins that could contain her energy, no dress that could survive her for long, no matter how hard she tried to be grave and solemn.

"Right here," I said, and put my arm about her waist. "You look nice."

"Like a liberated city?" she asked with a smile.

"Not really," I said. "But I'm not sure I get the point of that." Demetria had a part in the parade which she was very proud of, marching with a dozen other girls of good family her age as Liberated Cities of Asia in the pageant. Demetria was Miletus, a nice compliment, and one I was sure I should thank Bagoas for. She had a very elaborate headdress with buildings made out of gilded cartonnage. It made her look less like the city of Miletus and more like a fourteen year old girl in a funny hat, but she was very proud of it. "You're prettier without it," I said.

Demetria gave me a dubious look. Are a father's opinions of one's appearance to be trusted, particularly when he's an old man out of touch with modern fashion? I thought so. She had my dark hair, almost black as mine had been, and her mother's gray eyes. Alexander's eyes. She was the only one of the five children with Alexander's eyes, Demetria the youngest, the child of my old age.

"Don't you need to get going?" she asked. "Mother's going to take me to the staging point at the gymnasium before she goes to the reviewing stand, but don't you need to go to the palace first so that you can do whatever you're doing?"

"I do," I said. Of course I did, but I might savor another moment more with her. On a morning like this it seemed that the years had passed so swiftly. They were passing still. In a few short years she'd be married and here no more.

"The boys have already left," she said. Her older brothers both had places in the parade, Isidoros with his regiment and

Hephaistion with the ephebes of the city. "You're going to be late."

"You are as bad as Bagoas," I said, getting to my feet. "Hurry, hurry, hurry. I'll hurry to the palace and stand around a century waiting for your grandfather when I might have breakfast in comfort here."

Her eyes were grave. "Does he really mean to do it then?"

"What better time?" I asked lightly, but I also wondered. Could it be done? I knew what Ptolemy contemplated was no mere ceremony. I, of all people, knew that.

Demetria said nothing. She got to her feet and leaned up to kiss my cheek. "Good luck then," she said. "I'll see you in the parade. Well, I probably won't see you, because I can't actually lift my head wearing the city, but you'll see me!"

"I'll see you," I said. "You'll be perfect."

My litter was ready with my arms inside. They were too heavy to wear all day comfortably if I didn't have to, and for once I didn't have to. I would put them on when the time came. The bearers set off at a comfortable pace, and I opened the curtains to watch the sun rise over Alexandria.

The Canopic Way was cordoned off because of the parade, though thousands of people on foot hurried along with sun shades and baskets to stake out a choice spot to watch. The street cleaners had been out, and the streets steamed from the water burning off in the first sun, cleaned in the night by their pumps so that the stones shone white in the dawn. Every façade, every building shone. The turquoise and gold of the House of Ptolemy hung from public buildings and private houses alike, but no bunting crossed the street. The floats were too big. They would foul in the banners if any across the street were allowed.

I had to go by back streets. Even they were crowded. As we neared the palace we came close to where the regiments were to assemble, lined up in procession order. Hoplites stood about, sarissas in hand, gabbing and eating pockets of dough filled with fruit that an enterprising vendor was carrying about in a tray around her neck. They parted to let me through.

Getting through the guardpost took a moment, mainly because the Indian envoys from Bindusara were ahead of me in half a dozen litters, the nearest occupied by a nobleman in scarlet silks and his companion whose bald head and saffron robes proclaimed him a priest. I leaned out to call my greetings in their own tongue, and the priest replied in good Greek. "Good morning to you as well, General Lydias. A very auspicious day!"

"The gods grant it may be so," I replied before our bearers parted us. They were going to the reviewing stands for ambassadors, and I to Ptolemy.

It was no longer easy to enter the palace. Thirty five years had passed since I had first come here, thirty five years since Alexandria rose from stakes and string. Then it had been a sad excuse for a palace, a great bleak building with little to recommend it. Now it was a palace in truth. There was a warren of fine colonnades opening on inner and outer courtyards, gardens and seaward vistas, promenades lined with fig trees and fountains with statues of deities Greek and Egyptian alike. Isis stood beneath a pair of groomed apricot trees, a sistrum in her hand, while at her feet amid carven shells a great galley rose with a sterncastle like a cornucopia, Isis Pelagia, Queen of the Seas.

"Lydias!" Ptolemy said, coming across the colonnade, two attendants at his back.

"My lord." I bent my head.

He wore a turquoise chiton bordered in gold, but his movements were stiff and slow, deliberate rather than decisive as they once had been. How not? The man was nearly eighty-two.

I straightened up. "You truly mean to do this?" I asked.

"I do."

"It is not too late to simply honor the King," I said.

Ptolemy put one crabbed hand on my arm. "All very well for you to say," he said. "A strapping young man of sixty four! But no. I am certain." His eyes met mine, dark and keen as ever. "Don't you think I've earned some peace and quiet at my age?"

"Of course," I said. I glanced at his two attendants who stepped back out of earshot respectfully, as though I were a man to be feared. "But it's never been done, Manetho says. It's never been done, to call Horus Indwelling out of a living Pharaoh and invite him into the body of his son. It's supposed to be done with your body when life has left it. What will happen if we try to do this while you live . . ."

"I've had eight decades and more," Ptolemy said. "More than enough for any man. And you know as well as I that the work of the state has become too much for me. Would you have me linger on into my dotage, making chaos of the work of my life in senility? Philadelphos is a man grown, a man of full years and trained to be king, not a child heir or an unworthy son. It's time for him to be Pharaoh. It's time for me to put it down and let him take it up."

I shook my head. "I know that well enough," I said. "But for any man to take off the crown . . . How does one even do it?"

He smiled at me. "The same way he took it up. All improvisation." He lifted his hand from my arm. "Come, my friend. Manetho and Bagoas are waiting."

I raised an eyebrow. "Has not Bagoas enough to do with

the procession and banquet?"

"He does." Ptolemy looked amused. "He's been driving us all for days. But Manetho thought that if this were to work it would be best if the same companions stood with me as at the original ceremony all those years ago. And that would be you and Bagoas."

We did not go to a tomb, but rather to an inner chamber. Ptolemy was not a dead man. Instead, it was his office, the clutter and work put carefully away to make room for us—Ptolemy and I, Manetho and his two assistants, and as I washed my hands and face, Bagoas entered with Philadelphos. He caught my eye over the prince's head.

Philadelphos looked nervous, as well he might. He was a plain young man, brown haired and clean shaven, with a slight tendency toward pudginess inherited from his mother, Berenice. Later in life he might run to fat, but at present he looked ordinary and cheerful, like any young advocate or teacher. Well, any who in an hour might be Pharaoh of Egypt.

"Ready?" Ptolemy asked warmly.

"As much as ever," Philadelphos said. His brows knit. "I suppose I would be no more ready if you were really dead. But then the enormity would be eclipsed by grief. To invite a god into one's self, to share one's body . . ."

Ptolemy patted his arm, veins standing out in the back of his hands. "Horus isn't such a bad guest," he said. "And I should know, having shared with him for thirty four years. You'll get along. You're not too young."

Young to us, I thought. But we had been a decade younger when we conquered the world.

"No, Father," Philadelphos said dutifully with a doubtful

expression that looked exactly like Demetria. He was, after all, her mother's half brother.

Ptolemy smiled. "I'll have a few years yet, I hope. Time to raise cats and write my memoirs. That's worth doing, I think."

"May we begin?" Bagoas asked sharply. "There is still the procession and the banquet." And the other ceremony besides. No wonder Bagoas seemed a bit on edge.

Ptolemy took no offense. He had had decades of being ordered about by his chamberlain. "Let us," he said mildly.

The door opened to admit the two friends of Philadelphos who would stand as his companions, his trusted friends his own age who might walk through life with him if the gods allowed it, and the last priest who carried the ebony box containing the funerary tools.

Manetho looked around, and I settled into position at Ptolemy's right side, just as I had stood in the tomb at Saqqara all those years ago. Manetho looked little different, save sparer than ever. "We begin," he said.

In those days I had not understood the words. I had not spoken enough Egyptian to follow the phrases of the rites, and I knew little of their customs. Now I understood enough. These were the rites usually performed at a funeral, seventy days after death, to honor the departed and to release their ka to Amenti. They were abbreviated, of course. There was no need to reanimate each sense, sight and hearing and scent. Ptolemy had all his senses. There was no need to open his mouth or give him the breath of life. Ptolemy breathed still. He stood unmoving in his embroidered chiton, grave and solemn, a curious peace about his face. I wondered if he spoke with Horus within. I wondered what he said.

Manetho's voice quickened. "Come forth!" he said. "Come

forth, son of Isis! Come forth from the king who has been your host, from he who is now Osiris! Come forth, and dwell within this prince, this man prepared!"

Ptolemy let out a long breath, his eyes closing as though in concentration.

To the other side of him I saw Bagoas stiffen, his fine face going taut.

"Now," Manetho said quietly. "Sem-priest."

With the expression of a man about to plunge into water he knows is cold, Philadelphos reached into the open box and took out a dagger of meteoric iron, the same one that we had used so long ago to open the mouth of Alexander. He lifted it out carefully and his eyes met his father's.

"Go on," Ptolemy said evenly.

Philadelphos swallowed, and then lifted the blade so that the very tip touched his father's lips.

There was no sound, and yet it felt like a breath of wind through the room, as though every lamp guttered in a sudden gust. Philadelphos' eyes closed and he swayed as though the wind pushed at him.

And then all was still.

Manetho lifted his voice. "All hail Horus, Lord of the Two Lands! All hail Ptolemy Philadelphos, the Great House of Egypt!"

Philadelphos' eyes opened and he blinked, as ordinary and unassuming as before, himself and still himself. One of his friends let out an exhalation, but he did not know as I did how little it changed a man. And how much, though in ways that could not be seen.

Carefully, he laid the dagger back in the box and then raised his eyes. "I am Pharaoh," he said.

"You are, my son," Ptolemy said. He looked shrunken somehow, though he had not moved. Scarcely a quarter hour had passed, and yet without Horus indwelling he seemed smaller, frailer, as though that mighty power had held him up.

Philadelphos nodded. "Right. Then. Pharaoh." He had been bred for this moment, and yet it settled onto his shoulders like a heavy shield.

"Your coronation?" Bagoas prompted.

"My coronation." Philadelphos squared his shoulders. "Let's do this."

"As you wish, my Pharaoh," Ptolemy said.

The reviewing stand had sixty couches and a canopy of pure white linen overhead to keep off the sun. My couch was in the second row, as befitted a veteran of Alexander's army, a retired general of my years who happened to also be Ptolemy's son in law.

Chloe was there ahead of me, reclining on her elbow, her hair elaborately pinned up with pins in the shape of butterflies. She looked up pensively as I came down the steps. "How is he?" she asked, and I knew she didn't mean Philadelphos.

"He seems fine," I said, sitting at her knees. "He's not dead, if that's what you mean."

"I was afraid he would be," she said. "Only my father would have his own funeral while he's still alive!"

"He said he didn't want to miss the party," I said. I took her hand and squeezed it. "Really, he's well."

"And Philadelphos?" she asked. They were not terribly close, Chloe and this half brother young enough almost to be her son.

"He feels the weight of it." I looked out at the parade route, where the first troops were passing the review stand, horse archers in turquoise silk on prancing horses, musicians following them with trumpets and drums. Chloe and I could not have been heard at the next couch over that din. "But he will come to terms with it. He's as prepared as any man may be."

"I hope so," Chloe said, and then speech became impossible as the musicians drew near.

Behind them came the first cohort of the Elephant Corps, fine in their embroidered caparisons, and the crowds gave them a cheer. Elephants always make a fine show.

The first of the floats followed, Alexander and Ptolemy three times life size, gilded statues enthroned side by side, the founders of the dynasty. Alexander wore ram's horns on his head, and Ptolemy held a cornucopia on his lap like Serapis, pouring out grain.

Once, I thought, far away in a green land on the other side of the sea, there were two brothers born to a mountain chief, one on the right side of the blanket and one on the wrong. And now they sit enthroned as Egyptian gods.

Behind them maidens dressed in white emptied baskets of sweet cakes, tossing them into the crowd adorned with ribbons. Children scrambled to catch them, riches from the wealth of the Ptolemies.

Lest the generative message be missed, the next float was a giant phallus the height of third floor windows, painted gold and tied about with scarlet ribbons.

Chloe's eyebrows rose. "Really?"

I leaned close so that no one would overhear. "No one has a bigger one than the Ptolemies?"

"There she is!" Chloe sat up and pointed. Behind the marching hoplites that followed the giant phallus marched the Cities of Asia. Demetria was in the first row, stepping along with a look of concentration probably occasioned by her unwieldy hat. We shouted and cheered for her as any parents would, though of course she could not pick us out in the crowd, but I saw her tip her head as she passed the reviewing stand, smiling upwards as though the sun rested in her face.

And then she was past, down the street toward the temples.

"There's Hephaistion," I said. The ephebes had come around the corner on horseback. He was riding smartly, with less hemming and hawing and more staying neatly in line than most of the boys. A better rider, I thought, my heart filling with pride.

A page came up beside me. "General Lydias? Pharaoh . . . er . . . I mean, Ptolemy, would like to see you."

"Of course," I said, and got up leaving Chloe to cheer for Hephaistion.

Philadelphos sat on the throne, the double crown of red land and black on his head, his face a study in concentration. Ptolemy had the first couch to the right, the place of honor, and a page swept a fan to keep the flies away. "Come sit with me a moment," he said, and I did, aware of the honor. "What do you think of our parade?"

"It's splendid, of course," I said.

"And overdue," he said. "Long overdue." He squinted down the street and I saw what he saw, a sight once altogether too familiar.

Alexander's hearse rolled along for the last time. Pulled by forty oxen, it lumbered along, splendid as it had been the first time I saw it on the road from Lebanon, gilded victories at the corners lifting their wreaths to the sky. Splendid and beautiful, but it seemed antique somehow, a little off, as though it belonged to another era from the beauties that surrounded it. As we were.

"The final journey," I said.

Ptolemy nodded, and I saw him swallow the lump in his throat. "He was disembarked in the harbor before dawn," Ptolemy said. "The last stage of the road from Memphis. And now to his tomb in his city."

I had seen it, of course, many times in the last years, many times in the decade it had been building. It was a tomb to rival the famed Mausoleum in Halicarnassus, a confection of marble grander by far than the tombs of the Persian kings, than the tomb of Cyrus at Pasargadae, a tomb to fit Egyptian ideas of the grandeur due to dead kings but made as Greeks preferred, the perfect marriage of styles and splendors, as though the best of the lands Alexander had ruled were all laid at his feet.

Ptolemy smiled. "Gods, how you hated that funeral wagon!"

I laughed. "I did. It maneuvers like a barge!"

"Some other man's job today," Ptolemy said.

"Thank the gods."

It came closer and I came to my feet as one should in the presence of one's general. Within it, Alexander lay still as he would lie for all time in the city that bore his name. At my side Ptolemy came to his feet too, and a silence swept over the crowd. Here and there within it gray heads bent.

"Most of these children never knew him," Ptolemy said, his eyes bright.

"No, sir," I said. I had not either, not really. Perhaps he had spoken to me half a dozen times, half a dozen anecdotes told and retold. Yet I had marched with Alexander.

We stood, and the hearse passed.

"We have been in such a story," I said.

Ptolemy looked at me sideways. "Tell it, my friend," he said. "I mean to."

I shook my head. "I have no words," I said. "I am not a

learned man, and I cannot write this as it was."

"Perhaps in time you will find the words," Ptolemy said, and clasped my arm. "Find the words and tell the story."

The trumpeters played a fanfare. The hearse passed on toward the Soma. Another regiment of hoplites followed, eyes front. The elephants came on, the second cohort leading a float made in the shape of a great ship, Isis on her prow. I stood with Ptolemy under the endless azure sky.

PARADISE
641 AD

In a way, this is a Hand of Isis *story too—about our main character's return to Alexandria many years later, only to find Dion still keeping the flame alight.*

We watched them leave the harbor as agreed, ship upon ship of them. The siege was over, and if they wished they could go under safe conduct. For one more day they could go. Whatever was left after that was ours.

In the dawn light we rode into empty streets. Those who were left, the poor, the helpless—they stayed, cowered in cellars and prayed. I rode through empty streets, my horse restive, tossing her head and setting all her bells singing. I rode through white streets wider than buildings, past markets with their shutters nailed closed, past deserted houses, past strange temples with pointed monuments ten times the height of a man, past their churches. I followed my lord 'Amr ibn al-As through the city.

I had my orders that afternoon—to find out how the waterworks functioned, that it should continue to bring us water. We always think of water first. When you have never had enough, when you have grown up where water is more precious than gold, the first thing you consider is water, even in this bright place beside the green sea. I had my orders, and quarters in one of the palaces the Byzantines had deserted.

At evening I walked on the terrace. The sea wind kissed me.

Below, the harbor made a crescent of blue, as though I stood at the topmost point and watched it curve away to my left. Across, on the island, the mighty lighthouse greeted the dark, taller than anything I had ever seen, a mountain made by men long ago in the dawn of the world. How was it made and how did it work? That was someone else's duty. Mine was waterworks.

Beside me, fig trees in pots as large as a man bloomed in the twilight. Behind, there was a bathing pool. Water, blessed water in such quantities that a man could spend all day bathing, paddling about in a pool of clean white water! On a trellis that separated it from the terrace roses bloomed, their soft perfume scenting the air. The city gleamed white and pink in the sunset.

"My lord," one of my men said, coming onto the terrace. "This man says he must speak with you. We have searched him and he is unarmed."

I turned. He was past his prime but not old, with a trimmed grey beard and bright blue eyes. "What do you want?" I asked him in his tongue. It came easily to me, but I had only heard it a year or two, here and there.

He inclined his head smoothly. "My lord Mikha'il, I have come to ask you for a life."

I raised an eyebrow. "There are no prisoners in my keeping, and I shall take no prisoners in Eskendereyya unless someone offends against the law, for the Prophet said to treat the Egyptians as our kin."

"I am asking for life more dear than our kin. I am asking for our books," he said, and his back was straight. "My name is Eucherios, and I have in my keeping some thousand books that were brought to safety during the siege, when the buildings in which they had been housed from time immemorial were burned."

I frowned. "Are these sacred texts?"

Eucherios shook his head. "No, my lord Mikha'il. Not if you ask if they are Bibles. They are science, poetry, records—a little of this and that, whatever we could carry when the fire broke out. Many of our books were taken over the sea, but we could not in conscience leave people here and take instead books to Constantinople. So these have stayed, and I with them as their keeper."

"You are a brave man then," I said, one to another, "To stay in a city where you do not know what will happen for the sake of some useless pieces of paper."

"They are not useless, as you will see," he said. "I am told you have control of the waterworks. But to understand how they work you must read what I have."

"You can tell me the secrets," I said sharply.

He shook his head. "I can tell you how this or that gate works, where that plunge is. But you must learn the principles if you mean to truly use them. You must learn the science of hydraulic engineering. And for that you will need books. For that you must read."

I shook my head, pacing away. The sun had set, and over the harbor the last wild birds were flying, homeward bound, their black wings and white bodies against the sky, black winged gulls. The harbor was empty. Not a ship remained.

"To read," I said.

Eucherios stood behind me. "Yes, my lord Mikha'il," he said.

"And are you not afraid to come to me thus?" I asked. Most Greeks fear us. Yet there was no fear in his face, only a strange familiarity, as though I were greeted by a friend.

"No," he said. "An angel told me I will be safe."

I looked at him, but there was no deception about him. He believed what he said.

"You shall teach me," I said. "You will teach me to read, and teach me all the knowledge of this city."

His voice was amused. "That should take many lives of men, but I will teach you what I can." He came and stood beside me at the rail, looking out over the sea, the lighthouse against the sky and we stood thus for some minutes.

A whiff of perfume drifted over from the roses. "It is Paradise," I said, and for a moment wondered if I had not fallen in some battle and dreamed dying that I continued. "Paradise. I have died and gone to Alexandria."

SLAVE OF THE WORLD
1203 AD

If, in some ways, Georg is the worst of our main character, Jauffre is the best. Not since Lydias has he been soldier and priest at once.

It had been twenty years since Esclamonde had married someone else, twenty years since he had replied with a vow of perpetual celibacy, but Jauffre de Vallombreuse was still a handsome man. His neatly trimmed dark beard was threaded with silver now, accenting his temples where his hair swept back like the feathers of a hunting bird. His eyes did nothing to reduce that impression, raven dark under arching brows, with the fine clean lines of his face as beautiful as some ancient sculpture. He had stood, in Ascalon Outre Mer, for a sculptor who wanted his likeness for the Archangel Michael. He knew, without modesty, that it was entirely appropriate. He had thought the sculptor caught perfectly his long, swordsman's hands, and the touch of regret about the mouth. Clad in white samite, the cross formeé on his chest, a cloak of scarlet about him, Jauffre knew he looked every bit what he was, a Knight Commander of the Order of the Temple.

Behind him his godson, Laurent, cleared his throat. Laurent was fifteen, nearly ready to be knighted on his own, though he was not destined for the Order. Orphaned as a child, and the heir to lands, Jauffre had guarded Laurent's inheritance carefully until he should come of age. Jauffre was a younger son himself, and had had no such prospects. Which of course was the reason

Esclamonde had not married him.

Twenty years had passed since they had been boy and girl together, twenty years since one hurried kiss that he had held in his heart.

She had married, of course. Esclamonde had married a landed gentleman thirty years her senior. He had been in Damascus when he heard that she had borne a daughter. He remembered vividly sitting in the library, a copy of Ptolemy open before him, thinking that it had been five years. She had been five years a wife, five years that man's possession, while he had fought the Saracens and learned mathematics, traveled through the desert heat and over the wide dark sea. Five years.

He had been in Ascalon when he'd heard she was widowed. Twelve years. He was part of the Inner Circle then, one of the guardians of the treasures more precious than gold. He had touched them, once or twice, hidden gospels unearthed from buried amphorae, undestroyed by Nicea or any Pope since then. He spoke five languages now, Arabic as well as Greek and Latin and Hebrew, and his native Frankish. He could trace the paths of the stars as the ancients did. He had a copy of Arrian's Anabasis, copied laboriously himself, though he could not quite imagine what an elephant was, nor what Alexander wanted with them.

Twelve years. Wife and mother and widow, back in distant Aquitaine. It was hard to remember her face.

Seventeen years, and he had heard of her again when he came at last to Paris, Preceptor and priest. He heard she was a heretic.

And now she wished to see him, Esclamonde, Cathar Perfect, holy saint or heretic, or whatever she was now.

"Will you be going in, sir?" Laurent asked, still holding Jauffre's reins politely.

"Yes, of course," he said, removing his riding gauntlets and handing them to Laurent, while Laurent passed off the reins to the stableboy. A ruby ring glinted on his sword hand, symbol of his mastery.

And his stomach lurched.

Esclamonde was in the solar. Three young women sat near her, garbed in white like novices, mending in their laps. She stood.

Her dark hair was caught beneath a white wimple, and not a strand of it showed, but her eyes were as fierce and bright as ever. He had assumed that ascetics starved themselves, but Esclamonde had run a little to flesh, her breasts full beneath her gray gown. After all, she was only thirty-six.

"My lady," he said, bending in a bow.

"Jauffre de Vallombreuse," she said, and her voice was clear and keen. He would have liked to have thought it caught a little. "We are grateful that the Order has been so helpful with regard to the timbering conflicts we have found ourselves in."

"My lady," he said, straightening, "It is my understanding that those woods are yours, and that you hold them as your daughter's dower, per your husband's will. If you wish to timber, you certainly may." He met her eyes. "But surely you did not need me here to thank me for helping the resolution of your timbering case."

"Walk with me," she said, and took his arm, leading him toward the still garden. It was early spring, and there was little to see. The roses entwined, barren, on the wall.

Jauffre tried to keep his arm from shaking at her touch.

"You look well," she said, but did not look at him. Her white hand was unadorned on his sleeve.

"Thank you," he said. "Esclamonde . . ."

She turned and faced him, rosemary bushes on either side fragrant where her skirts brushed them. "I sent for you to save you."

"To save me?"

Her eyes roved up and down him. "Jauffre, look at yourself. Sword at your side, a man of blood instead of peace. Wearing white silk and jewels, traveling the world. How are you living in the spirit?"

"I am a priest," Jauffre said, but he felt the color rush to his face.

She shook her head. "A priest should be humble. Should strive to separate himself from the things of the world. And you, who have traveled the world, what have you found? Riches?"

Jauffre inclined his head. Once, he should have ached. Once. "The greatest riches I have found are not jewels or silk, but knowledge." He grasped her hand, led her to the bench beneath a leafless tree. "Esclamonde, there are wonders I cannot even begin to describe! How can I show you in a few words what the river Nile looks like, winding through the Delta, or sunrise over Jerusalem when the gates of morning open? Or what it's like to swim in Caesarea, and see the ancient wrecks waiting just below the surface, the curve of an amphora just out of reach?" Her hand was warm in his. "I can tell the circumference of the world, and what India is. I can read poets no Christian has ever heard of, converse with Sufi sages, find the road to Palmyra beneath the desert, walk the chariot tracks of Timothy. I have watched the night in Bethlehem and mapped the skies."

He stopped then, for there was too much to say, but she only looked at him sadly.

"You are the slave of the world," she said. "And you know nothing of love."

With a jolt he remembered Charles in the desert, dying with

his hand in his, Baudoin singing with his clear boy's voice, and Rolf, whom he had dared to touch, once. There were others. The woman in Bethlehem who had skittered away, afraid that he would kill her for nothing, seeing something larger than a man in his face. William, standing beside his king, once and always true.

"I think I know something of love," he said. "If not love such as we might have shared."

Esclamonde turned away, and for a moment he thought a blush rose in her face. "Love is pain," she said. "Only the pure love of Christ is real, and we can only reach it by simplicity. By purging ourselves of pain and desire. Do you not see how you are enslaved?"

"By love for the world?" Jauffre put his head to the side. "By love for our fellow humans, no matter how flawed and rough they may be?" He put his hand on her arm. "Christ did not stand apart, but ate and drank and lived with his friends, not as a hermit in the wilderness. He did not enjoin us to abandon the beauties of the world, but to love as he loved, each lily in the field and star in the sky."

"They are illusion," she said, and in her beautiful eyes he saw an endless valley of pain. "There is pain, which is the world, and the absence of pain, which is heaven."

"The absence of pain is oblivion," Jauffre said grimly. "You are teaching misery, Esclamonde, you and your friends. And do you not understand that in spreading this heresy you are dooming these people? That you are dooming the peasants who work your lands to the cross when the Church has had enough?"

Her face was serene. "It doesn't matter, don't you see? We strive and we hurt and we die. And then there is the absence of pain."

"If you keep this up, it will be flame and sword," Jauffre said. "Esclamonde, I will not be able to protect you. The Order will not be able to protect you. There are currents in Rome. And we do not have the influence we once had. If you continue to spread this heresy, you will bring the suffering I have seen in Outre Mer home to Aquitaine."

"The suffering you have caused in Outre Mer?" Her eyebrows rose.

"I do not claim to be innocent of blood," Jauffre said. His fingers closed on her arm, blood red ruby winking. "I have never claimed that. But I have caused as little as I could. And I have never flirted with disaster as you do now. This dream of yours will condemn thousands to the fire!"

"We shall not cease to live for fear," she said, and took her arm from beneath his. "Nor will we cease to seek purity. You, with your silks and gold, your books and your bloodstained hands, you sicken me!"

She turned and walked away, her head held high.

Jauffre closed his eyes. Lord Most High, he thought, she will burn and there is nothing I can do. And how was it that I loved her? And how, oh God, that I still do?

LITTLE CAT
1012 BC

A little more than a century has passed since Gull stood with Neas
and watched a little coaster come into the dock, watched Markai
come home to his family. The seas have been scourged by raiders and
cities burned. The population of the Mediterranean has dropped to less
than half of what it was and in Greece literacy itself has been lost.

But no dark age lasts forever. Settlements away from the sea have
begun to prosper again, hill farmers with herds of goats and small towns
that are growing again into cities. And in these lands people have begun
to say, "Give us a king!"

However, Egypt has endured. Battered and humbled, the Black
Land stands still, temples and libraries, palaces and fields less than they
were in Gull's time, but not destroyed either. New peoples have settled
there, melting into its rich tapestry. One of them is a girl named Kadis,
and with her the soul that was Gull's returns to Egypt as she promised.

The gods walk the earth among men when they will, and
from time to time take a hand in the game of jackals and
hounds that they play; we know this in Nubia, though they
have forgotten it in Egypt. Perhaps they do it only for sport, or
perhaps it is because of some terrible compassion. Either way, it
is little comfort to the pieces, moved or knocked down by their
whims, like markers on a board.

I am the wrong person to tell a story of gods and kings. I
am not a scholar or a general, not a prince or a magician or even
a priest. I am an animal trainer, like my father before me. If I

had not been, I would have never left the Black Land, never met Baalthasar or Marah or Jonathan. And whether that would have been better or worse, only the gods can tell.

For three generations my family were archers in the service of Pharaoh, in his border wars, before my father took a different path. His brothers were archers, but his eyesight was too dim to shoot a falcon on the wing, and so he was apprenticed to one of the trainers of the great hunting cats that the lords of the Black Land love.

Thus I was born in the city of Elephantine, in Upper Egypt, where the Black Land borders Nubia and the river rushes out of the gorges and cataracts on its way to the sea. It is from Elephantine that the great cats come, and they are trained there before they go north to hunt beside lords and kings. I was my father's first child, and he was only half there when I was born. I was born the same day that his finest cheetah whelped.

It is a rare thing for a cheetah to whelp in captivity. They do not mate well when they are under the leash, because the female will lead the male a race across the desert or plains, only capitulating at the end, when he has pursued her day and night without water. In captivity, they often do not mate at all. And if you release a female in heat, usually she will never return.

Sakah did. She escaped when her time had come, but three days later she returned to my father, tired and footsore, her business accomplished. Her kittens were born the same day I was. They were infinitely more valuable, for even though I am freeborn the worth of a girl child is much less than even a single starred kitten of one of the great cats.

My father ran back and forth between the house of his mother, where we lived, and the kennels, where Sakah was. She bore four kittens, three female and a male, and my mother bore only me. It was because of this that they named me Kadis, Little Cat, in the language of Nubia, joking that I was the fifth kitten, the lucky one.

They had three days to laugh, because on the fourth day my mother took ill with a milk fever, and she died on the tenth day. I do not remember her at all. I wish sometimes that I did, but perhaps it is better so. You cannot miss what you have never known.

What I do remember of my childhood is good. Motherless, my aunts and grandmother doted on me. My uncles were older than my father, and they did not live with us, though four of my cousins did. My eldest uncle had died in a skirmish with the Melawesh in the far off Delta, and my aunt and her children lived with my grandmother as well. They were all four boys, the oldest nine years my senior, and the youngest the same age as me to the season, so I did not lack for family or love.

Gahiji, the youngest, was more like my twin brother than anything else, so alike were we in looks and temper. Like me, he was tall and clean limbed. We children of the desert tower over the men of the delta, and like the animals we prize, we can run day and night under the sun and the stars of heaven. Like mine, his skin was dark and fine, his eyes tilted and almond shaped. But where his eyes were dark brown, mine were almost golden, the color of honey or Sakah's dappled pelt.

It was Gahiji and I who were always in trouble. Once, when we were six or so, we stowed away on a river boat bound down the Nile to Thebes and then to Memphis. The sailors discovered us in a few hours and put us ashore at Tati, where angry and worried my father found us the next day. In the meantime, however, we had had a scare of our own, and decided that being without dinner and without a place to sleep was perhaps not so much fun as it might seem. By the time we were hauled back to Elephantine, striped from my father's belt, we were very sorry indeed.

It was then that my father decided that Gahiji needed something to occupy him during the day. He was sent to the school at the Temple of Thoth. Each morning he would leave with his bit of pottery and chalk, his lunch tied up in a linen cloth, to spend all day sitting with the other boys and learning how to write. In Egypt it is not only the children of the nobles who do so. Most freeborn boys learn at least a little for a few years, enough to keep accounts and understand contracts and sales. But girls do not go to the Temple of Thoth.

I was jealous, lonely, and wild to learn. Also, I imagine my grandmother found me a nuisance in the house, bored all day and missing Gahiji. Before the season ended she had convinced the scribe who taught Gahiji to let me join his class. I was five years there. I loved it and would have stayed if it had not been for Pharaoh.

My father was summoned to Thebes to bring his hunting cats and serve the throne. It was a very great honor, and a marvelous chance for him, so I did not doubt that he should take it. I was sorry to leave the temple, my friends and my grandmother, but I was also excited.

Gahiji was angry that I was going. "You will never come back, cousin," he said. "You will forget us in the North."

I shrugged. "I will not forget you. It is you who will forget me. Someday when you come North as an archer and a soldier you will walk past me in the street and not know me."

At this he brightened considerably. "That's true," he said. "I will have my turn. I'll be an archer, and you will still be a girl!"

My father and I left Elephantine immediately, walking along

the Nile on the way north. We did not take a barge for the same reason we did not use horses or donkeys – the cheetahs do not like boats, and horses do not like them. We had two cats with us, both females about a year old, sisters from the same litter. They were fairly well trained, but to sit quietly on a barge was beyond them. It took us two weeks upon the road before at last we saw the capital.

I was born and bred in a city, but not such a city as Thebes. It stretched as far as the eye could see on the eastern bank of the river, temples and palaces and great markets crowding for attention, houses of two or even three stories built of mud and brick, fields green with the harvest and the water gleaming sharply in all the irrigation canals. The palace came right down to the water, and rows of shapely trees along a stone embankment showed where there were pleasure gardens. At the flood the river must come right up to the top of the embankment, but now, at the harvest, there was a drop fully a man's height to the water.

Across the river, on the western shore, the docks of the temples on the riverbank gave to the red hills and the valleys of tombs. Ancient and white, the temple of some long dead Pharaoh glimmered. The sun sank beyond the hills, leaving the riverbank in shadow beneath a sky of purest blue.

We had quarters waiting for us in one of the alleys behind the palace. We did not go there, however, but instead directly to the menagerie at the palace where we would settle the cats. It was a neatly build brick building inside a courtyard with a high wall. My father nodded approvingly at the wall, which was twice his height and too high even for our nimble hunters to leap. Inside, there were three big box stalls and two enclosures. Clearly this had formerly been a stable for breeding. At some time past bars had been affixed to the windows. Some of them, like the walls, showed claw marks. There were no other animals there any more, however.

We settled the cats in as night fell. They were restless. I thought that no matter how well cleaned the place had been it still smelled of other cats to them. And perhaps we were also still in scent of the royal stables.

"We shall stay here tonight," my father said. "I do not like to leave them alone this way."

I nodded. "I'll get some bedding for us to put in one of the stalls." It would be too chilly otherwise.

One of the local trainers was hanging around. "I'll send a slave to bring you some food from the kitchens. There is meat for the cats, but you will want something for yourselves."

The slave brought not only bread, but a pot of beer and some fried fish crispy with breadcrumbs and savory with spices. My father and I sat back against the wall and had our dinner while the cats snarled and purred over a big sack of pig guts that had been provided for them. Outside, it grew dark.

"My daughter," he said, "our life is good."

I grinned and leaned back against the sun warmed wall. "It is. And I can't wait to explore Thebes and see the great temples, even the palace itself!"

He nodded mildly. "You will be careful, for Thebes is a great city, not a glorified provincial town like our Elephantine. And you will be careful in the palace, for palaces are always beds of intrigue."

"That sounds exciting," I said.

"You think so now. But you have not seen the power of kings to punish and destroy," he said. "Go sometime to the place of public execution and you will see what I mean and learn caution. It is best to serve kings well, but not closely."

I shrugged. I would have liked to have seen the king at least. Pharaoh Menkheperre was an old man, and Nubian like us. He was the grandson of that Piankh who had restored order to Upper Egypt in the wake of great disturbances, and his dynasty had held the throne for seventy years now, first his son Pinedjem, then his elder grandson Masaherta and now his younger grandson. Menkheperre had reigned both as High Priest of Amon and Pharaoh for forty years, and he had sons and grandsons aplenty to follow him. The royal family was huge, and the nursery that had in some times past had held only a single frail heir was now full with the grandchildren and great grandchildren of Pharaoh. After trials, the Black Land prospered. As it should.

I saw Pharaoh once, at one of the great festivals in the year after we came to Thebes. He was carried through the streets to the Great Temple of Amon at Karnak, and I went to watch, standing with the other children in the crowds along the street. He was an old man. I could not tell, as he was sitting in a litter decorated with gold and with palm leaves, how tall he was, but the skin of his face was wrinkled, and he held the crook and flail stiffly, as though his joints hurt.

And yet people cheered him. Menkheperre was loved. In his youth he had forged a treaty with the Other Pharaoh, Psusennes who claimed the throne in the North, in Lower Egypt. For fifty years Upper and Lower Egypt had struggled, each claiming that their Pharaoh was the legitimate ruler, each claiming the entirety of the Black Land. Menkheperre had agreed to a treaty line, and each Pharaoh had married the other's sister. Now they were brothers in law, and their heirs were twice kin. If we were not one kingdom as we had been in the old days, we were not a kingdom torn by war.

Each year the river rose and fell. Each year brought a new kitten or two for training. I worked with them at some length, pacing them and training them to go after decoys with teeth and claw, teaching them to stand on a lead and to wait. Much of what our cats must do was wait. They were to stand beside Pharaoh's throne at audiences and look fierce, the very soul of the Black Land.

I also learned to shoot a bow.

This was the fault of one of the young Nubians in Pharaoh's guard. He was a distant relation by marriage, and so when he was posted to Thebes my father invited him to dine with us. His name was Zuka, and he was sixteen.

I wondered at the time that he should volunteer to take me to the edge of the desert to shoot. I did not expect young men to waste time with me. I had forgotten that I was growing older. At thirteen I was tall and slender, small breasted and light on my feet, the sort of girl he would marry in a year or two, when he could support a wife. Of course he was thinking ahead, eating with my father and spending time with me. I understand that now.

What I knew at the time was that he praised my aim. My arms grew strong from drawing his compound bow, and it was not long before I could shoot well and swiftly. "It is in your blood," Zuka said, finding a reason to put his arm around my shoulders to correct my draw a little. "You are the daughter of many fine warriors."

"If I were a boy I should be a soldier," I said. "I would like to go to the lands of the Meshwesh, and north to Ashkelon."

"I have been to Ashkelon," he said. "And it is not so fine. And it is not ours anymore. The Peleset hold it, and if we come we must come as envoys. They took it with great burning and looting a long time ago."

"Not so long," I said. "I have seen the inscriptions. That was in the Second Ramses' day, and not even two centuries have passed since then."

"That is a long time," Zuka said. "When you compare it to the length of a summer's day. There are days that should last forever."

I laughed. "Maybe there are."

He was handsome, with his shaven head and fine body, but I was not moved. Though I was tall, my body was still the body of a child, and my heart was not ready to call any man my brother. And so I did not understand why he sulked a little when we returned to my father's house, and did not smile at me.

In due course of time perhaps I would have married him. But it was not to be. In the winter, at the height of the growing season when I had just turned fourteen, my father returned from the palace greatly upset.

I brought him water, and sat him in the shade. I knelt beside him and waited until he would speak, for he was almost speechless with what he had to say. At last he reached for my arm.

"You are a good child," he said. "And you do not deserve this misfortune."

"What misfortune?" I said. Fear struck me, but at the same time came the thought that he could not have displeased Pharaoh too badly and be allowed to return to his home lamenting, rather than being flung into prison or executed. "How have you displeased Pharaoh?" I asked.

"I have not displeased him, daughter," my father said, and he took another long drink of water. "I have pleased him, and that is worse. He says my cats are well behaved and beautiful."

"So they are," I said. "But how does this constitute misfortune?"

"He has determined to give a pair of them as a gift to some petty king of the Peleset with whom he wants to trade for precious woods. I am to go accompany them and tend them, while an ambassador presents his compliments and seeks a trade. This is a misfortune beyond belief! That I should be sent from the Black Land into this kind of exile for as long as the cats shall live!" He lamented further, and took another drink.

Then he shook his head and squeezed my hand. "I will miss you, daughter. I had thought to see you married and happy, and perhaps have a grandchild on my knee."

I gasped. "The cats will not live so long, father. Five years, perhaps, if the pair you choose are not too young when you go. And I am not old! Besides, where do you plan to leave me? I cannot stay in Thebes alone!"

"I will send you back to your grandmother in Elephantine," he said. "She will be glad to see you, and will find you a good husband while I am far away. For five years is a long time at my age, daughter. And who knows if I will ever return from that uncivilized place?"

"Surely it cannot be so bad," I said, remembering all I had learned of those lands at the temple and from Zuka. "They were ours once, not long ago. Ramses the Great conquered them, and Thutmose."

"They're not ours now," my father said. "They belong to the Peleset. There is some petty king who has emerged in the valley of the Yordana River who controls the forests and hill country. Menkherperre does not make war like Ramses. He seeks trade. And I do not doubt his wisdom."

Neither did I. Times had changed. I had learned that at the temple. In days past our chariots were our strength. Now it was our archers who defended us from Peleset and Meshwesh armed with strong iron. And once, long ago, there had been no chariots and no horses. Our oldest scrolls and pictures showed this – Pharaoh going into battle on foot, armed with a long spear.

"I could go with you, father," I said. "I would not mind seeing Peleset lands. And it will not be for so long."

He shook his head. "Kadis, that is foolishness."

"Why not?" I asked. "I do not want to go back to Elephantine. I could come with you. You are not going to the ends of the earth, but only to places that are well known and where we have long had trade. And you are going with a king's gift. You will be an honored guest, not a man with no means and no status. Why should I not join you there for a few years until you may return home? Why should I not see the world too? Besides, you'll need some help with the cats, and there is not a boy here you will want to bring."

My father smiled. "You are the jewel of my eye. I have been too indulgent with you, and have treated you too much as the son that we never had. You are right that there is no boy here who has half as much skill with the cats as you do."

"I can help you," I said. "And it is just for a few years. It will be exciting." I put my hand on his knee. "Remember, if I were a boy I could be going to war."

Then he laughed. "You know you will get anything you want from me, as always, Kadis!"

"You know I will miss you if you make me stay," I said. "Truly, father. I want to go with you."

He hugged me tightly. "And I would miss you. I suppose you may come. And I do need the help with the cats."

VESUVIUS
79 AD

*L*ong ago, Neas dreamed on the beach below Vesuvius, dreamed of fire in the sky and a burning city, dreamed himself looking back. Here is the other end of that dream, in which Marcus Gerontius Tasso dreams of Neas.

Marcus Gerontius Tasso was twenty-six, a soldier, a sailor, and a child of the East. His grandparents were Etrurian, certainly, under Roman rule for centuries, but his father had gone out to the East in hopes of making money, now that all those ancient lands were part of the Empire. And he had found what he sought. Importing fruit was a lucrative business. Dried dates, apricots, peaches and sesame paste were all important produce that shipped from Caesarea in Judea to the rest of the Empire.

Fruit importing was not for Marcus. He was the oldest, and his father's heir, and so of course he was the impractical one in a practical family. Both of his younger brothers were better merchants. He was the one with wild dreams of glory, of duels with Parthian champions and night marches across the desert. He was the one who was like his mother.

Now he stood on the deck of his ship, standing out from Stabiae, watching the world explode. The sky was on fire. Mount Vesuvius rained ash and pumice down on them, even so far away, and the morning sky was dark as twilight. Dark clouds rolled down the slopes of the mountain, swallowing greenery and vineyards, houses and livestock and people. Already he could see fires in the towns, Herculaneum swept under. He had been here on leave, two years ago with his parents when they were in Italy. He had stayed in this town, been a guest in these homes.

On the next ship he heard Admiral Plinius giving the orders. They would sail into the gates of the underworld and take off as many survivors as they could.

He gave the orders and the rowers picked up the beat, the ship going forward. Pieces of pumice floated on the surface of the sea like scraps of papyrus. Burning stones rained down. He ordered the ships boys to have buckets of water at the ready when they landed on the deck. He was doing twenty things at once, everywhere on the deck, watching the town coming nearer.

And then, for a moment, everything was still. It seemed to him that the town was gone entirely, not engulfed in fire and lava, but never built, that green lands curved around the bay, three black ships drawn up on white sand beaches. They were little ships, less than half the size of his trireme, fragile looking. People were sleeping on the beach. Except for one man. On the nearest ship a tall man was looking straight back at him, light brown hair held back with a leather thong, bare-chested and strong. His blue eyes met Marcus' with a jolt.

Fire, and a burning city.

There were swimmers in the water.

"Careful with the lower bank!" Marcus shouted. "You there, get some ropes over. By Jupiter, this isn't an enemy fleet action! These are our people, the ones we've come to rescue! Careful with the oars!"

A young man about his age was treading water, a naked baby

held above his head. Marcus threw the rope himself, waited to see if he would get it. It slithered near him in the water, and he bobbed up and down, but at last got it. Marcus towed him to the side, but he couldn't climb with the child.

"Tie the baby on!" Marcus shouted down over the din. He hauled the baby up the side, then dropped the rope back down, but the man was gone. They were drifting closer to the docks. He hoped the man had gone up some other rope, but he couldn't wait to see.

"Get the lower bank in!" he yelled. They were going to break their oars against the stone wharf.

There was the strangest sense of unreality to it. The light in the sky, the burning world. The double image of the peaceful beach he had seen. Getting swimmers aboard from a burning city . . .

It seemed like days later that they put out again, racing against the black clouds that flowed down the mountain, a firestorm, a smothering blanket of ash. It was probably less than an hour.

"Row!" he yelled, "Pull for your lives!"

One of the ships was burning. Burning stones had caught her.

"Row!" Their decks were crowded with people, some of them collapsed on the deck, retching from the fumes. Fifty? A hundred? Out of how many thousand? Out of how many people he had known, how many shopkeepers from streets he had walked, girls from the taverns he had visited?

Out to sea the skies were clear and it was morning, the pall of cloud rising like a column.

It was not until they were well out to sea that he realized he was still holding the baby. Marcus looked at it dumbly.

It was a little girl five or six months old, and other than

a long red burn down one arm, she seemed to be all right. Big gray eyes watched him solemnly, clutched against his left shoulder.

Well, Marcus thought, his mother would know what to do. He held it and went aft to set a course for Capri.

UNFINISHED BUSINESS
22 BC

The German bodyguard, Sigismund, is one of the few characters to survive the ruinous end of Hand of Isis. *He's retired to Rome, gotten married, and runs a tavern in the Subura. Nothing strange will ever happen to him again. Or so he thinks, until a Roman waif named Lucia enters his life with her strange dreams . . .*

I dreamed, and in my dream I drifted like smoke through the streets I walked waking, through the neighborhood and away, and up the steep cobblestone streets of the hills. It was a night of rain. I saw him then, just ahead of me, a man alone in the hours before dawn, his dark cloak pulled tight against the fog. I hurried to catch up with him, and he looked back, almost as if he felt me, a handsome face grown heavier with age. He stopped outside a great house, the two bodyguards on duty coming to attention, but he dropped back his hood and I saw them relax.

"Yes, sir," one of them said. "The lady is expecting you." The porter opened the door behind them and he passed in.

I hesitated at the threshold. Beyond, I could see the wall shrine, masks glowing in the light of a small lamp, left lit all night. I wasn't sure I could pass, or what would happen if I did.

One of the masks, crudely made of wax with distorted features, as though made by a child's hands from memory, looked straight at me. "You may pass, friend," it said, and I drifted in, insubstantial as night mist.

They were already speaking, standing in the dining room,

the empty couches pushed against the wall for cleaning, their voices low and urgent.

"He has doubled the offer," the man said quietly. "He is inclined to take it. After all, it's something for nothing."

She shook her head and looked away, her hair pinned up and fully dressed even well before dawn. "It's too far, and she's too young. The other children need her. She's still a child, really, and Juba is too old. I should know. I was married at that age to a man much older, and while he was kind to me I was not happy in it. I will tell him no, that it cannot be done."

The man took a deep breath, and took both her hands in his, looking into her face. "I tell you that it is better if you do this. Better that she be far away in Numidia when Helios puts on the toga."

Her eyes did not leave his. "You can't think that."

His hands tightened on hers. "If I did not think it, I would not take the risk of telling you this."

"He wouldn't."

He held both her hands and said nothing until she could no longer meet his eyes.

At length, she broke away, pacing around a little table. Her voice was still low. "Why are you here, Marcus?"

"To keep faith with the dead," he said.

She paused, her fingers running over the inlaid surface. "I will send her then with many blessings. I have loved them all, you know. I have loved her, though I think she does not thank me for it, proud as she is. It was a year before she would let her brothers eat before she had eaten and an hour passed."

He looked at her and said nothing, simply met her eyes as she glanced up.

"You cannot really think it," she said.

He seemed to be choosing his words carefully. "And how should you prevent it, if he wanted it?"

She took a quick breath. "Is Africa safe enough then?"

"As safe as anywhere in the world. And anywhere would be safer than Rome. Juba is not a very young man, as you say, and he needs his bride alive. There is little point in marrying the last Ptolemaic princess otherwise." He stepped forward until they almost touched, the little table between them. "You know he marched in Caesar's Triumph when he was seven years old."

She took a hurried step away, half turning from him. "Marcus, how did we get here?"

"One step at a time," he said grimly.

I related the entire dream to Sigismund the next morning, perched on a tall stool while he was wiping the counter and tables down. In the kitchen, I could hear Mucilla getting the ham in the oven, basted with honey and spices, so that it would be ready for the dinner hour. It was what the tavern was known for. The sign over the door might be a smiling pig, and everyone in the neighborhood called it The Happy Ham. My parents didn't mind too much, as long as I only took off to the Ham twice a week or so. They knew Mucilla was a good woman, and since Baby came there were seven people in a one room apartment, so getting rid of me for half a day was just fine.

Sigismund said nothing, but his quiet got deeper as he scrubbed off the counter.

"Don't you think that's strange?" I asked. "I thought the lady looked rich and pretty, though she was much older than Mommy."

"I think you shouldn't tell those dreams to anyone but me," he said. He didn't look up.

"I wonder who the girl was they were talking about," I said, kicking my feet. "Another kid. Someone who's in trouble." I leaned my elbows on the bar. "Sigismund, do you think we could help her?"

Sigismund looked at me sharply, his bright blue eyes flashing. "Lucia, I think you'd better forget it."

"How can I forget it? I think she's in trouble. Maybe we could help her!"

Sigismund threw his cloth in the bus pan. "Lucia, you are seven years old!" He came and bent down to me on the other side of the bar. "I'm a broken down old veteran with one arm, and you are a child. There's no good that can come of meddling in something like that. I'm sure the Lady Octavia can take care of her."

"Octavia?" My ears pricked. "Then you know who those people are?"

Sigismund threw back his head. "Argh! Why did I say that?"

"Who's Marcus? And who's the girl?" I put my chin in my hands, my elbows on the counter. "You believe me, don't you? You believe the dreams are real."

He sobered, and beneath his bushy eyebrows his eyes were troubled. "I do," he said. "I think you dream true. Sometimes the gods touch someone and they alone know why. But you are too young and too small for the things you're reaching for. Grownups die for meddling in this."

I looked at him levelly, though a chill ran down my back. "I'm not scared of that."

He looked away, and I thought I saw him shiver as he reached for his cloth to begin wiping the cups. "Then think about how it will affect people around you," he said. "Doesn't your father talk about why you live here?"

I shrugged. "Not really. I know once there was money, when he was a kid, but now there isn't."

Sigismund picked up a cup, bracing it against the stump of his right arm, and cleaning inside it with the other hand, his back to me. "Your grandfather was a client of Marcus Antonius. When the Antonians went down, they went down hard. Your grandfather died bankrupt, and your father works odd jobs as a clerk and lives in the Subura. If you start saying this stuff, people will think you got it at home. You could get your dad into a lot of trouble."

"Oh." I hung on to the edge of the bar while the horror ran through me. Something bad could happen to Baby, and to Lucilla who toddled around on her little feet tearing up the apartment, and to my brother Lucius, even though he was nine and could already read and figure. I wouldn't want anything to happen to them. And I loved Mommy, even if I always felt there was something strange, something wrong about having them be my family, as though they were very nice people I'd been sent to stay with for a little while. And Dad was nice too, thin and harried and always working until late. I would never want to get them in trouble.

Sigismund put the cup down, his face softening a little. "Now I served with Marcus Antonius." He gestured toward the stump of his arm. "It was Antonius himself that put his shield over me, when I lost this arm in Parthia. I've nothing in the world against Antonians. But things are what they are, and they're not going to be changed by an old veteran who runs a tavern and a little kid who doesn't come up to my waist."

"Oh." I considered this a little while, watching him wipe cups. After a while I leaned on the bar again, putting my chin in my hands. "Sigismund, do you think I'm strange?"

He looked at me, and I saw he wasn't really mad. "Why do you ask?"

I shrugged. "Mommy does, sometimes. She said I was strange the other day, when I was telling Baby a story I made up. Not like she was mad at me, but because she thought it was weird. I mean, I made it up. That's all!"

"What was the story?" Sigismund said, bracing a cup against his stump again.

"Once upon a time there was a little prince," I said. "And his evil uncle wanted to kill him. So he sent a magic snake into his room at night to bite him. But the prince's mommy had a faithful dog and cat . . ."

With a clatter, Sigismund dropped the cup, and it shattered on the floor. He swore.

I stopped, looking at him. "Why is that story bad? I just made it up."

Sigismund bent down and picked up the pieces of the cup. I couldn't see his face. "I heard someone tell that story to a little boy a long time ago, in a house just across the river. Twenty years ago it must be, now."

"Who?" I asked. The cold along my spine clung now, but I wouldn't not ask.

"A beautiful woman I used to know," he said, still muffled by being down behind the bar. "A woman I knew a long time ago."

He stood up, the broken pieces of the cup in his hand. "She was very clever, and very loyal, and I think the gods touched her too." He looked at me, and his blue eyes were piercing, as though some thought had suddenly occurred to him and he was weighing it for the first time. "There are a lot of strange things in the world, and who can fathom the gods?"

I swallowed. "What happened to her?" I asked, though I thought I already knew.

"She died," he said. "Seven years ago on the third day before the Ides of Augustus, four months to the day before you were born."

I couldn't look away from his eyes, and the chill ran down my arms, all the way to my fingertips. "Sigismund, do you believe that oaths are stronger than death?"

He couldn't look away either, or he would have. "Yes," he said. "And may the gods curse me if I ever betray my friends, living and dead. I'll look out for you, Lucia. That I swear on the memory of the men I fought beside who are all gone now. That I swear."

THE MESSENGER'S TALE
1553 AD

*T*his *story was written for my friend Tanja Kinkel, who inadvertently inspired* Hand of Isis, *and now asked me for a story about Elizabeth I of England. I'm not sure this is quite the story she expected!*

The great did not dare speak of it, as though saying it would compass it, or should at least render them suspect and complicit in what might then seem a crime. But in the kitchen we knew, as we had known these months, that King Edward was dying.

I am no one in particular, Dickon my name, and I am a groom who would be a man at arms, would that I were a man, not a boy of sixteen. But that will come in time, mother says, as it always does, barring evil. It may be that I do talk like a magpie, but I can hold my tongue when need arises, and that is the cause of this tale. Otherwise I should just be one more boy about court, enthralled by the fine horses and the bright swords, slipping up to the gallery that I might lie on my stomach and look through the rail at the bright masques as I did last Christmastide, when the masque was King Alexander and the Queen of the Amazons. I do love such, and perhaps I should be a player instead of a man at arms, did I speak better and less!

But I can hold my tongue at need. Though I do not know how Cecil should know this. It is said that he has the measure of men, which I believe, because before that day I do not think we had exchanged three words, save over the mounting of a horse which I held for him, and how I shortened his stirrups while he waited.

My mother knew of course that the King lay dying, and she wept and prayed for him in the kitchen. It was sad, she said, to see a boy so close to her own in age, him being but a year my junior, who she had known from infancy die so long and painful, and with none who loved him to mourn him, only ambitious men who already plotted and planned. His Popish sister Mary would not mourn him. And the other sister—well, none had seen the witch's daughter in a long time. Who was to know what she might do? Perhaps it was she who cursed him to wither away, though my mother said such talk was foolishness.

There was less to do in the stables than might have been that night. With the king ill, there were no hunts or pageants, and the great lords in attendance had brought grooms of their own, so I had not so many horses to have a care of. It was raining, thunder shaking the sky, and I went into the kitchen as soon as I was able and stood about warming my backside at the fire while my mother had one of the girls take up a bowl of thin gruel and milk that the king might eat. It was quiet enough. In a bit, my mother went up herself, to talk to the nurse and see if she might how the gruel had gone, and if an egg posset would be welcome. I sat down on the hearthstone. A great gray cat had wandered in from nowhere, and stood purring before me.

"There now, Puss," I said, petting her. She looked fat and happy, and I supposed my mother fed her, as well as there being good hunting in the storerooms. I should have gotten up and gone back out, but she climbed into my lap, kneading, and I thought I should stay a while. Her green eyes blinked at me.

There was a clatter on the stairs, and Cecil plunged in, his somber doublet out of place in the kitchen, black velvet like a

Spaniard. He looked about a moment only, and his eye fell on me as I came to my feet right enough, dumping the cat on the floor.

For a moment I thought he would go back out again, but instead he raised one eyebrow, as though he were neither surprised nor pleased. "You, boy. Your name is Dickon?"

"As it please your lordship," I said.

"Do you know the way to Hatfield House?" he asked.

I nodded. "I do, my lord." Which was falsehood, but I can find anywhere, right enough. And how hard could it be?

He shoved a piece of paper into my hand, folded but not sealed. "Take this there, now. Give it into the hand of no one save Mistress Ashley's charge, and say nothing of it. If you do, I shall call you liar."

"Yes, my lord," I said, and took it, putting it safe in my jerkin against my breast. "I'll be off now, storm and all."

"Good lad," he said, and pressed a coin into my hand. Like a shadow, he was gone as though he had never been in the kitchen.

I read it of course, in the stable. You'd not think the likes of me could read, but I'm cleverer than I look, and all in all it was a simple thing, three lines long, the ink trailing off across the page on the last word, as though strength had given out.

Sister
Do not come. They will kill you.
Love

Standing in the warm stall beside a good mare, Rosamund, I felt a chill run down my spine, for now I knew all. As I saddled Rosamund up for our run into the night, I knew I carried the King's last word to his sister, handed by Cecil to a man he knew nothing of. Inside, there were men who would pay for this piece of paper, but I do not think I truly considered it. He was my king, you see, a boy my own age who my mother loved, and though I was no knight or gentleman, and he should never know my name, I should do what I had promised.

How hard could it be to find Hatfield House?

"North on the Great North Road. Ye can't miss it." The directions sounded simple, but less so in the face of the storm. I had never seen the like. It had been only a bit past ten when I left, but the night seemed to go on forever. Soon London was left behind in the mud flung from Rosamund's hooves. Once we were out of the city I let her go, and she ran as if the hounds of hell themselves were behind her. Perhaps they were. In the driving rain and the thunder, perhaps they ran behind us.

It would have cost nothing to have stopped and waited out the worst of the storm, but I could not, and she caught my urgency. We must ride. We must outrun whatever it was that followed. Another messenger? Messengers bearing tidings of the king's death? Death itself? I did not know, but we ran, Rosamund and I, through the night and the storm.

There was no one else on the road, cutting clear and straight through the forest, unnaturally so. Even the ruts only went a few inches deep in new laid mud, and here and there I heard the ring of her hooves on stone. Old ways, my mother called them. Roads laid imperishable from the beginning of time.

Lightning cut across the sky, a single flash illuminating. In the middle of the road ahead there stood a massive black dog, his mouth opened in a snarl.

Rosamund shied, and I fought to stay on her, her distress bugled to the sky. The dog growled and charged.

And then we did run as though the hounds of hell followed us, off the road and into the underbrush.

I fought her. "Get back on the road!" She did not heed me, running panicked through the trees, and it was all I could do to stay with her.

Behind, the hound bayed, calling the others of the pack, and I heard the huntsman's horn echoing over the crack of thunder. The Wild Hunt, in full pursuit.

I should have prayed. I should have . . . something. But all I could do was hold to Rosamund, and hope to stay on, and hope that she would not fall.

The sound of the hounds was louder, and I almost felt their breath as a dog snapped at my ankles, barely missing in his leap. Rosamund spun about, darting like a deer down some track. Her hooves left the ground as she jumped a fallen tree, and still I clung to her, my cloak half over my face.

The hounds bayed after.

And why should they, some part of me wondered. It was not one of the dangerous days. None of those were in July. What had roused the Wild Hunt? Surely nothing less than the passing of a king.

Ride, something whispered in my ear. Ride as though the fate of Britain rode with you . . .

Behind me, the great hounds bayed. The rain flew at my face with a thousand icy claws. The lightning split the sky.

Rosamund went up on her hind legs with a whinny of pure terror. I pitched from the saddle, and I fell hard against the muddy grass, half hauling myself to my feet as she plunged away into the night.

The hounds bayed, and I ran through the forest, hearing them always behind me, now closer, now farther. I suppose the rain put them off the scent somewhat. But where should I find shelter? Behind me, they were tireless, and it was hours until dawn.

I blundered into a dense thicket of evergreens, then out again into a clearing. Something glimmered whitely before me, a well half overgrown with climbing vine. I seized a broken branch from the ground, turned to face the dogs, and as I grabbed it I knew what it was, rowan.

"Back!" I yelled, brandishing it before me. It gleamed blue silver in the lightning's crack, and in the sudden flash I saw it rightly, a sword in my hand.

"Back!" I yelled again, and the dogs halted. Light ran down the blade, as though it had been dipped in moonlight.

The leader of the dogs snarled, but came no closer. Then, with a last growl, the pack turned and fled into the forest.

I sank to my knees in the muddy grass, my chest heaving. I could think of no words. I bent my head to the ground.

"Water for you, swordsman," she said.

I raised my head to see her holding out a cup for me, a maiden dressed in white, her hair pale as silk across her shoulders and her lips as red as berries. Her gown was white, and there was no touch of rain on her face or her dress, though I was sodden through.

I looked at the cup she held for me, and some bit of mother sense penetrated. "What's in it?"

"Nothing that will hurt you," she said, and a smile flickered across her lips. "Water from the well."

"I would not drink from death," I said. I should fear her, but I could not, though my whole body shuddered.

"This is not from that river," she said and held the cup for me.

I drank. It was clear and cool and sweet, as water that springs from deep underground on a summer's day. I drank deep, and it seemed I had never tasted anything so rightly, so completely, as though my entire self were knitted whole.

"Thank you, Lady," I said. "If by your power the dogs were called off."

She shook her head a little sadly. "Not by my power, swordsman, but by yours. I fear I have but little power outside this grove, away from the well. You see, no one believes in me anymore." She glanced at me again, and beneath her smooth maiden face I thought for a moment I saw something much older, something in her eyes.

I shook my hair out and tried experimentally to stand. "Still, you have my gracious thanks," I said.

She took a step away from me, one hand reaching down to caress a broken bit of worn marble. "This was once a shrine on the Great North Road. Kings worshipped here, and lords out of Spain and Africa, men who brought their horses and their vines, their loves and their dreams." She looked back at me. "And their nightmares too. But they are gone, and I am here." She glanced up at the trees that arched above, and the sadness in her voice made me ache. "I can still be here."

The sword was still real in my hand, steel hilt wrapped with leather. I looked at it with less wonder than I should have. "How did I do that?"

"Turn a stick into a sword? Face down the dogs of the hunt?" She sounded amused. "Because you are a servant of this wild magic that runs through the land, older and stronger even than tales of the hunt. That magic was old when the Normans came to these shores, when Northmen and Saxon raiders plied their longships, old when the Romans came with their vines and their gods, older and stranger, a wind through the world that cannot be commanded." She half turned from me and then looked back, her face framed between her hair and her shoulder. "A thousand years have passed since that wind last swept through Britain, since the last echoes of that song faded with blued blade slipping into blue water, to sleep in the lake."

"Or sleep in the hollow hills," I whispered. "Is that what has happened, that those knights have slept a thousand years?"

She laughed, and her voice was like the ring of steel. "Do you think they have nothing better to do?"

"I don't know," I said, but I did know, even as I said it. I could see the plunging ships and the wide ocean of the north, swan prowed ships cutting through gray waters, ever westward. I could see the walls of Ascalon Outre Mer rising in sunset while I stood, red cross blazoned on my chest, coming home. Too fast to name, too many visions, the queen of the troubadours with her amazons about her, and the virgin warrior heaven sent, too many others.

Before that, a swift Arab mare beneath me, I gazed on the city of my dreams, her streets half ruined and her temples gone while my song of victory turned into ashes in my mouth. I had wandered her streets then, looking for I knew not what, and in the turn of a corbel, in the shape of a stone had suddenly known her, had embraced her as a man who has traveled the world and come home to find his family in poverty will reach for his mother and lift her from the gutter.

She was smiling at me.

"What was that cup?" I asked.

"Not the river of death," she said, and smiled again with her mouth like cherries.

I shivered then. "And what should I call you?"

"Nimue will do," she said.

I thought a moment, then phrased my question carefully. "Why would you help me? If, as you say, this magic is outside your touch."

She turned, and her eyes met mine, dark as the blackness between the stars. "Because the tide of blood is rising. The Templars could not stop it, nor Joan, nor the lords of Grenada in their power and beauty. Soon that tide will wash over this England, the tide that has turned sacrifice to misery and love to pain, and this new world will die aborning. This wild magic is our hope, this wild tempest through the world that has no remedy. In this fatal thing must we place our trust." She raised her chin, and for a moment looked nothing more than a young maiden, uncertain in her pride. "And I do trust in you, Dickon, whatever face you may wear. Bear that message to your princess, Knight Companion of the Round Table."

I did not ask how she knew what I carried. But as she leaned toward and put her lips to mine, I fainted and I knew no more.

I woke when a shadow fell across me. I lay among the roots of an oak tree, and Rosamund stood beside me on the wet grass, her long horsy nose snuffling at me a little anxiously.

Cautiously, I sat up. I was soaked through, and lay where I had fallen when she had thrown me the night before, or at least I supposed it the place, as little as I could tell in the storm. I should have felt ill. A man cannot take a bump to the head and lie all night in the rain otherwise, but I felt as hearty as ever in my life.

Rosamund whuffled at me, and I hauled myself to my feet against her side. "We had a run, didn't we, girl?" I said. "Such runs as stories are made on. Now let us see if we can walk."

She nickered softly, and turned to drink from a well half choked by the greenery around it. I bent, and pushing away the tendrils of plants, cupped my hands in the water. It was no more than a small, cool spring, but in the stones I thought I could make out still some worn letters—RPINA. I shook my head. I had not then come far from the Great North Road. I must find it and be on my way. If I poured the water from my cupped hands with a thought, that was no more than country superstition, which is allowed to such as I.

I reached Hatfield House before noon, though Rosamund took up lame a half mile from the gates. So I arrived hat in hand, leading a lamed horse through the mud, and no doubt looking more like a beggar and less like a mythical knight in disguise. I had half convinced myself that it was no more than mad dreams. I had ever loved the stories of King Arthur, and no doubt my mind ran wild, with the storm and the fall and all. A foolishness, but not harmful. Nothing of which I should ever speak to anyone. I had resolved it all a dream.

"I have a message for the Princess Elizabeth," I said boldly. "A privy message, and I can give it to no other."

The men at arms looked suspicious, but they did at least send for a groom for Rosamund, and escort me into the solar, where a somberly dressed woman looked up from her needlework.

"I am Mistress Ashley," she said. "You say that you have some message?"

"I am to give it to the Princess Elizabeth," I said. "I have risked my life in wind and storm to carry it now, and I must place it in her hand."

"From what man has this message come?" she said, a wrinkle between her brows.

"That I may not say," I said, trying to stand straighter and look less like a stable boy and more the sort of man who might be entrusted with the fate of nations.

Her brows rose. "The Princess does not receive messages from unnamed men. You will give it to me."

"Your pardon, Mistress, but I will not."

I do not know what she might have said, had not the door opened.

She had come from the garden, and a few strands of red gold hair escaped from her cap. There was color in her cheeks, and her slight form swayed like a bell in her heavy skirts, rose and cream together. "Kat, what is this?" she asked, and her eyes when they fell on me were brown, not pale as one might expect.

Mistress Ashley was exasperated. "A messenger, My Lady. Naught but a stubborn boy who says he will give his letter to no hand but yours, and will not tell me who sent it."

She gave me a quizzical half smile, crossing the floor to me. "Then give it to me, man. I am the Princess Elizabeth."

"With all good will, My Princess," I stuttered, trying to draw it forth from my chest. It was a little damp, but I thought it was still readable. I put it in her hand, trying not to touch her fingers. To touch her would be like touching fire.

She took it, and spread it open. I saw the color rush to her face, and then she paled, reading it once, twice. Wordlessly, she handed it to Kat Ashley. Her eyes snapped to me.

"Do you know what this says?"

"Yes, My Princess," I said.

"And you know who wrote it," she said.

"Yes, My Princess," I said.

"And who gave it to you?"

"Cecil, My Princess."

She turned and walked away, stopping halfway across the room before the windows, bright lit with summer sunshine, then pacing back. "Are you Cecil's man?"

"No, My Princess," I said. "I was to hand, I think, and he did not want to make a great fuss. My mother serves the king."

Her brows rose again. "In what capacity?"

I felt a furious blush rising to my face. "She's a cook, My Princess."

She did not laugh. Instead her eyes met mine, as though looking for something there. "And who do you serve?"

"You, My Princess," I said.

In one movement I sank to one knee, my hand reaching out to her. "I, Dickon son of Robin do swear to you with my life's breath, to be your own true man in all things, waking and sleeping, in war and in peace, in prosperity and doubt, to obey your word and hold your honor above all else, guarding you with my body and soul while life and breath last!"

I thought that Mistress Ashley looked aghast, and perhaps she should, muddy boy of sixteen on his knees to the witch's daughter, this girl scarcely nineteen who could hardly expect to live out her brother's funeral. And yet I felt no doubt at all.

She took my hand between hers, and her long fingers were cool against my wrist. "Then I do accept your service and your sword, Dickon son of Robin, that you shall be my true man and that I shall stand as your liege in all things, and be as generous as I may. For I will have need of you, and do accept your service most gratefully, while life and breath last."

The sunlight slanting through the roses outside touched us like a benediction.

MORNING STAR
469 *BC*

There is a full novel about the Persian princess Artazostre the daughter of Darius, Lioness, which I hope to sell in the future. Alas, this scene will not be part of it, as it takes place long after the end of the novel! And yet this story ties books together. The young naval officer, Artontes, will one day be the grandfather of Artashir in Stealing Fire.

This story is for Rachel Barenblat, who has faithfully and helpfully reviewed so many of my books before publication!

"The Most High and Noble Princess Artazostre, widow of General Mardunaya, First Among the Thousand. The Most Noble Captain Artontes son of Mardunaya of His Gracious Majesty's Navy. The Most Noble Lady Epyaxa daughter of Mardunaya. The Most Noble Lady Stateira daughter of Mardunaya."

The Greeter called forth his words in a clear voice, rapping the butt of his staff twice on the floor at the end, bronze ringing. We walked between rows of nobles live and carved, the faces on the wall echoing the courtiers before them, a riot of colored silk and rich perfume, oiled curls and glittering jewelry, myself in front with Artontes just behind and to the side, the girls following. Stateira's eyes were huge. She was eleven, and this was the first time she had been presented. Children are not, but she was a woman now, and in her first grown up dress she walked beside her sister, her chin so high I doubted she could see anything besides the ceiling.

At the end of the row, a change in the stone parquetry of the floor was our signal, and as one we all sunk into the prostration. I could not see the girls, but from the corner of my eye I could see Artontes, graceful and handsome in his crimson silks, the prostration an act of beauty to behold. I, of course, did not go all the way to the floor.

"Rise, dear sister," the Great King said, and I looked up to see his mouth quirk at me. "All may know that you are welcome to Our court whenever you desire to make the journey."

"It is a pleasure, Majesty, to make the journey for such a happy event," I replied as we all got to our feet.

"Indeed," he said, and his eyes were on the girls behind me. "It gives me great joy to celebrate the marriage of my niece Epyaxa, and to wish for her the blessings of a long and fruitful life."

"My thanks, Great King," Epyaxa said behind me.

His gaze shifted. "Captain Artontes, you are just come from Our Ionian fleet?"

"I am, Your Majesty," he replied. "From Naxos, where I am stationed aboard the warship Avenger."

"We thank you for your service," he said. "And may that service be as long and valiant as that of your late father."

"I only aspire to my father's achievements, Your Majesty," Artontes said. "I do not hope to duplicate them." It was his stock answer, I thought, polished to perfection. After all, had he heard anything else since he joined the fleet other than will you be your father again?

My brother's eyes fell on Stateira. "And this must be my youngest niece. When I last saw you, you were a child, not a beauty."

He meant to be kind, but Stateira gulped. "It's nice of you to say so, Your Majesty," she almost whispered.

He glanced at me, and I gave him the look which said, no, nothing is wrong, only shy.

"You are welcome to Our court," he said, falling back on the formula. She would be easier, I thought, once she was away from this great crowd. In truth, this exchange did not mean so much.

Afterwards, in the private hall behind, my brother came and embraced me. "You're looking well," he said.

"So are you," I said, and I thought that it was true. Yes, he had gained some weight, but it gave him dignity. There were a few threads of gray at his temples, but he looked fit and somehow more settled, as though he slept at night without ill dreams. Which would be a trick in this palace.

Only perhaps not. While he greeted Artontes again I looked about. It was an inner hall with no windows, so it could not possibly be actually lighter than it had been. It was instead the air of the place, as though sadness no longer pooled in corners, darkness lying under the furniture waiting to leap. It felt clean. It felt new. Somehow it was different.

I had tried before, but this palace had defeated me, too much weight of pain and misery still lying here, too many miserable people in too small a space, drowning all in sorrow. Too much had happened here.

Miletus was nothing like this, nor Ecbatana where Anahita watched over us. Even Babylon was not like this, even the new palace in Persepolis was not quite this bad. Pasargadae was the heart of it, the place all the bad spread from. And yet something was different.

I was trying to feel what, to trace the walls of this place with my mind as I so often had as a child, and did not hear my brother when he spoke until he touched my arm.

"Artazostre? I want you to meet my new wife. I told you I remarried, but I know you haven't met her yet."

I turned, a polished smile on my face, though my mind was still half wandering.

She was tiny, almost a head shorter than I, with long dark hair worn up in intricate pins and combs ornamented with sapphires, a great star sapphire set in silver resting across her brow. Her eyes were dark too, warm and limpid, and her flawless complexion was alabaster touched with gold. "I hope you will let me call you sister too," she said, and embraced me to give me the kiss of peace.

It is her, I thought as she touched me. It is her. This warmth, this light, they emanate from her. I thought it, and my lips touched her cheek in greeting.

He had promised it, the winged messenger Mikhael. He had promised I was not the only one who labored, though I might not see the other workmen. He had said they were there, that the peace of our empire was a great task, for all our subjects in all their lands were uncountable, and when the Great King spoke thousands might suffer or be instead redeemed. Do you think, he had said, that all such rests only on you? You labor alone, but you are not the only workman.

I squeezed her hand a little too tightly, but she smiled as she stepped back, a beautiful, mild smile that had steel beneath it. "I am so glad to meet you," I said. "It is clear that you do my brother good."

My brother beamed at her, his arm around her proudly. "I have no need of any other, concubine or wife, while I have her with me. She is my Esther, my Morning Star."

TEMPLAR TREASURE
1188 AD

*N*ot all treasure is gold and jewels. For centuries people have speculated on what the mysterious treasure of the Knights Templar was. Jauffre de Vallombreuse, who was once an oracle named Gull, discovered it for himself.

"Jauffre de Vallombreuse?"

I raised my head. I was keeping the morning vigil in the chapel with two others, and there was no reason to interrupt me, unless upon high authority. The vigil schedules were set by the Knight Commander.

The squire who had called me was seventeen or so, nearly on the verge of knighting, but I did not know him well. He served Master Raimond de Genlis, who was more than a Knight Commander indeed. He was the Seneschal of Beirut, and I had only spoken to him twice. "My master would like to see you, sir."

With a quick genuflection to the altar I got up and followed him through the garden and along the rampart.

Master Raimond stood looking out at the sea, the curve of the cornice slicing like a crescent through the deep blue. I bowed as proper.

"Jauffre de Vallombreuse," he said, and it seemed to me that his voice was thready. He was, after all, quite old. "You have presented an interesting conundrum to the Order."

"I have?" I had certainly tried to do no such thing.

"You are a fine horseman and a dogged fighter, with some good tactical sense, they tell me. As such, you would go far commanding one of our outposts, or leading an advance force against the Saracens." He looked at me keenly. "But unfortunately you also have a mind. I am given to understand that your Latin is passable?"

"So Sir Hugh tells me, sir," I said. Most knights could not read or write when they were received, no more had I. And why should we? Our business was the horse and sword, and an area no more than a day's ride from the place of our births. We should never see the sea, nor anything but the peaks and valleys of Haute Savoie.

But I had been gone from there six years, quite a lot of time to learn, even through some battles. And Latin was incredibly easy.

"And I am given to understand you speak Arabic?"

"I have picked up a bit, sir," I said, "For the marketplace and the like."

"Because Knights Templar spend a deal of time in the marketplace." His eyes twinkled. "No Greek?"

"Just a few words with this Byzantine or that, sir," I said. "No more."

"I see," he said, and this time the amusement in his voice was unmistakable. "Which is the conundrum. Were you intended for the field, your path would now be clear—a transfer to some fortress more likely to see action than Beirut. And were you feeble in body but keen in wits, it would be best for you to retire to the copyist's work. On top of which I am given to understand that you have a damnable sense of curiosity. What is this business of you wandering about the stones of the old Roman baths?"

I swallowed. That, at least, I knew I should not have been doing. "I wanted to see how they were constructed, sir. The arches seem too long for the weight they must have borne, and I wanted to see how it was done."

"And did you discover it?"

"No, sir," I said.

"I suspect you have not the mathematics," Master Raimond said, and met my eyes when they sought his. "There is a gentleman named Euclid who might prove of assistance to you, were you to meet him."

"I should be delighted to meet any friend of yours," I said courteously.

Master Raimond laughed. "Come then, Jauffre, and I will introduce you to another friend! I think he may prove more to your liking than Euclid!"

Slowly, he led me into the seaward tower, where I had never been as the first floor was the province of the copyists who did not like soldiers stomping through. He led me up the long spiral stair, stopping often to catch his breath, until at last we came to the uppermost chamber.

The room was octagonal, with windows in four faces to catch the light. Each window was set with dozens of panes of glass, worth a king's ransom. One window was open, and the breeze from the ocean blew through, teasing a piece of paper on a table, the tassels of a scroll on the shelf. Four walls had windows. The others had books. There must have been a hundred books in that room, some of them locked in covers of leather and precious jewels, others only scrolls, cased in white linen. There was nothing else in the room, save a copyist's table and chair and lead weights for holding paper flat.

The room and its contents were worth more than every

horse in the stable, every sword in Beirut, every ring and chain.
I caught my breath. "A hundred books . . ."

"A hundred and eleven," Master Raimond said. "Most of
them discovered here, or in various places nearby, some quite
literally dug out of the ground." He looked at me keenly. "You
have doubtless heard that we guard a priceless treasure."

I nodded.

"This is part of it. This is a granary, Jauffre. The things
contained within these books are precious seeds, and if you read
them they will change you. You will no longer be the man you
have been. Think upon that before you open them."

I nodded again sharply. "I am not afraid, Master Raimond."
In truth, my hands were itching.

"They will challenge your faith, your beliefs about the
world, your sense of all that is right and proper. They will open
windows into a different earth just as surely as if you went over
to the Saracens and dwelled in Babylon."

I met his eyes. "But if the things I believe are right and true,
then what fear have I of challenge, for will those things I learn
not simply prove what is? And if the things I believe are not
right and true, would it not be better for me to know that and
face it like a man?"

Master Raimond laughed. "I see that you will enjoy this.
Yes, joy, Jauffre. There is something to be said for joying in
work well done. Spend the morning with my friend, here. And
come and find me in the afternoon that we may discuss it." He
took down a carefully wrapped bundle, opening its linen case
and stretching it gently on the table, the paper darkened with
age but still readable. "We will talk about copying later. Today
you can just read."

He put the weights on the corners, and I sat down, bending

over the spidery Latin. "Read for me, Jauffre."

The Latin was not hard. I cleared my throat. "The Anabasis of Flavius Arrianus. Wherever Ptolemy and Aristobulus in their histories of Alexander the son of Phillip have given the same account, I have followed it on the assumption of its accuracy . . . ."

WINTER'S CHILD
1821 AD

*S*ometimes *a character who is only peripheral in one book wants a story of their own, one that gives a different perspective on the main characters. This is not a story of our main character, Gull etc, who doesn't appear until almost the end, though the events of this story were in many ways set in motion by her. This is the story of her granddaughter, a very brave little girl, growing up in the funeral games of the wars of revolution.*

I wrote this one for my friends Kathryn McCulley and Anna Kiwiel, who have both contributed so much to the Numinous World over the years.

The first thing Natia remembers is cold, cold and her mother's arms around her, almost as cold as the rest of the world. In her childhood she was always cold and it was always winter. Now that she is a grown girl eight years old, she knows it's not always winter. She can remember last summer. It was warm some of those days, and she helped in the gardens at the abbey. Some of the sisters were kind to her and wanted to teach her about plants. Weeding and tending the herbs in the abbey's garden was a chore, but it seemed like a game to her.

She was out in the garden when her mother died. She was working among the stones, carefully rearranging the edging of the beds where the birds had disarranged it, when it seemed that suddenly a huge hush came over the world. The birds stopped singing. The soft rustles in the grass were stilled. Even the clouds stopped moving. Natia knew. She knew in that moment that everything was different, that a strange peace turned on a still point.

One of the sisters came to get her. She washed her hands and they took her in. Her mother lay still and silent in the only occupied bed in the infirmary, her hands clasped around the rosary on her breast, her pale blond hair loose around her shoulders like a girl's, the oil still glistening on her forehead. Natia knelt beside her. It was all still quiet. She had known her mother was dying for years. She was seven and a bit, and entirely alone in the world.

In her childhood it was always cold. She wonders, now that she is eight, if it felt like that when her father died. She does not know. Perhaps he died before she was born. Probably. That's what her mother told her, what her mother wanted to believe. Natia doesn't entirely believe it, but she has always pretended that she did. He froze to death, her mother said, on his way back to us. He never saw you, but he loved you before you were born. Never forget, she said, whatever came afterwards, that you were the child of love.

Natia has no picture of him. Her mother never had one. She has no memory. Sometimes she looks at her reflection in the glass windows of the convent when the light is behind her and her features reflect, remembers her mother and tries to see what is different.

Her mother's face was rounder. Even though Natia is a child there is a sharpness to her chin, to her nose that isn't like her mother. Her eyes are a different shade, not pale blue-gray, but dark blue, the color of shadowed pools. Her hair is not ice blond, but darker, like warm honey. Someone else has stamped themselves on her, someone else is there in her bones. Her mother was short and deceptively fragile looking. Natia is tall for her age, and her hands and feet are long. Who had these eyes like wildflowers? Who had these big hands?

He must have been tall, she thinks. He was tall and good looking, and still so young. Her mother said that he was eighteen and she was seventeen that glorious summer of 1812.

Natia is the child of war. Everyone hates the Russians, even the priests. Everyone hates that Poland is no more, that they are not free. Everyone remembers that for a little while they were.

Your father was a hero, the sisters said to her soon after her mother began coughing blood, soon after they came here. They were all heroes, the brave young men who died for Poland, whether or not they were Polish. Her father was Dutch, and he served the French Emperor, they said, but he died for Poland.

And because of that they do not ask too many questions about whether her parents were married. Her mother says they were, that they spoke their vows to one another even though there was no priest, even though he was Protestant. Natia doesn't know whether that counts or not. She thinks when she was younger, before they came to the abbey, that people called her bastard. Back in Warsaw, when her mother cleaned houses and she lived in the scullery. She doesn't remember that very well. She doesn't want to. She was always cold and always hungry.

The sisters give her food. Mostly it's the same bread and soup they eat, but they never tell her she can't have any. She can't remember who did. Someone, once. Someone when she and her mother were both very hungry.

Now she is alone. She hears the sisters talking, hears them discussing her with Father Andrzej when they don't think she can hear. There are so many children who need charity. There are so many poor, now that the Russians are back. They do not want to keep her if there is somewhere she can go, if there is someone who wants her.

"She's too pretty," one of the sisters says. "She will be preyed upon in service, even if we find her a place in a respectable house. The girl will be a beauty. And she is too young to take care of herself, too innocent."

Natia thinks to herself that she's not. She has never been innocent, whatever that means. She remembers what it was like just before they came here, when her mother had the men. She remembers being told to stay in her bed with the covers up and not look, no matter what she heard. She looked anyway. Lots of times. She could peep through a fold and her mother wouldn't see. She remembers the sweating and the struggling the men did, the coins they left.

She looks at her face in the window and wonders if she is pretty enough to find someone who will take care of her, someone who will not die. But how do you know who will die?

Winter. The washbasin freezes over at night in her room. The snow forces the shutters in some of the rooms downstairs, breaks a stained glass window in the chapel with its weight.

Father Andrzej has written a letter. "Your mother," he said. "I asked her when she was dying if you had any kin. She said that your father had said that his mother still lived in Paris. She must be an old woman, if she is alive. But I have written to colleagues there. Perhaps someone can find her. Perhaps . . ."

Perhaps she has money, Natia thought. Perhaps she will want me. Some old harridan half a world away. If my mother had thought she would help surely my mother would have written to her. And perhaps she too is long dead.

Cold. The days lengthen, but the world is frozen in ice. They say it is the worst winter since that one, the winter before she was born, when the bravest sons of revolution froze in Vilnius or died in the Berezina.

A letter comes with the first thaw, and Father Andrzej is happy. You are a fortunate girl, they all tell her. You are going away from here. You are going to Paris.

Natia wants to see the letter. Father Andrzej shows it to her, but she can't read it. It's in French. "Does she say she wants me?" Natia asks.

He temporizes. "She says that she knew your father intended to marry your mother, and that she met your mother once. We will send you to her."

"Does she know I'm coming?" Natia asks.

"She will when you arrive," he says.

And now it is spring. At the first false thaw she is off to Warsaw with Father Andrzej. He leaves her there at another house, and then she is on her way to Munich with Father Wicus, a much older man who has no time for children, but who will take her as far as that. He does not talk to her, but at least they have seats inside the carriage. It's very cold still.

Her birthday comes the day they arrive in Munich. She is eight years old.

That night she sleeps in the infirmary of a convent there. There is no one in the infirmary, but there are no other beds. She dreams of having a kitten who would curl up on her feet. She wonders if the old lady will be very strict, and if she will beat her. She wonders if people will call her bastard in Paris.

A few days later she is on the way to Frankfurt. Three young seminarians are going there, and she is to go with them. The carriage is dirty and wobbles a lot. The seminarians ignore her and drink more than strictly necessary to keep them warm.

They don't want a little girl. The carriage doesn't stop until late at night.

Natia falls asleep looking at her reflection in the window, watching shadows move on the glass. Sometimes she dreams about distant places, watching shadows move. Sometimes she can see mountains and seas in her reflected eyes.

One of the seminarians is going on to Strasbourg. He is kinder when his friends are gone. She has a few words of German and he has a few words of Polish, enough to say that he has a sister her age.

Natia looks out the window and sees that spring has come. On this side of the Rhine the trees are blooming and the land is greening. Birds are soaring in the sky, singing absurdly.

He teaches her a few phrases of French as they roll along. "Bonjour, Madame Grandmere." That is what she must say when she meets her. She practices saying her father's name aloud. "Sous-Lieutenant Francis Charles Leopold Ringeling." It sounds so very big.

She wonders if there is a big gloomy house with the windows all draped in black, old servants shuffling around in perpetual mourning for the Young Master, an old woman with rings on every crabbed finger who will think her very stupid because she does not know any lessons.

At Strasbourg she changes to a Flying Coach. She wonders if it will fly, and then is told that just means that they change the horses at posting houses. There is an old priest who doesn't speak a word of Polish who is supposed to take her along. She can't understand anything he says and he can't understand her. Nobody can. The only thing she can say is "Bonjour, Madame Grandmere" and "Je ne parle pas Francais." He buys her bread and cheese at the posting stops.

A woman passenger who is very pregnant gives her a handful of raisins and smiles at her, showing Natia her sewing. It's a baby's gown in thin white cotton. It might be finished before the baby comes. Natia wishes she could talk to her, but smiles are the only language they have.

She is asleep when they come into Paris. When she wakes they are already moving through crowded streets. They stop somewhere there is an inn or a posting house, and the priest gestures for her to get out. The woman passenger smiles at her and says something to the priest. Natia can't understand it, but the priest calls over one of the stableboys and gives him a message and a little coin. The woman pats her arm and smiles, saying goodbye.

Natia waits in the muddy stableyard. She has a little bundle and she stands next to it so that it won't get lost. The priest has gone inside. He is talking to people and drinking in the public room. Natia thinks it's not a good idea to go into public rooms. She thinks her mother told her not to, once long ago. Probably because she's pretty. So she waits outside instead.

There is a sudden disturbance at the entrance to the inn yard. An open topped carriage is stopping and a woman getting down. She's wearing a fashionable bonnet trimmed with feathers, and she's dressed in rose, not the pale kind of pink Natia thinks of as rose, but the dark rich saturated pink of real roses opening in the sun. She has a short jacket and gloves, but as she steps down Natia can see that her boots are black and scuffed, low heeled and meant for walking. The innkeeper and the stable boys are all running to do her bidding. She turns, and her eyes sweep over the yard.

Now that Natia sees her better she's not so young. The hair visible under the bonnet is gold, but her face has lines around her mouth and eyes, and there is a long scar across her forehead over one eye, clear and white as a sword. Her eyes are dark blue. When she moves she walks like a man, like a general must walk, a stable boy running ahead of her into the inn. She takes off one glove with a snap.

The priest comes tumbling out, hurriedly wiping his mouth. He tries to bend over her hand. They are saying something, and the priest doesn't like it.

And then the lady in pink turns and walks straight to Natia, who stands perfectly still, her bundle in her hands, and the lady kneels down to face her in the mud.

Natia gulps. "Bonjour Madame Grandmere," she says, and then stops, her French completely exhausted.

The lady takes Natia's hand between hers, the gloved and the ungloved, and says in perfectly clear Polish, "My dear Natalie! I am so glad you've come to live with me! I know that we will be very happy."

For the first time in long months, the first time all across Europe, Natia cries. She can't help it and she doesn't know why, she doesn't know how to bend gracefully into the lady's arms that go around her, how to cry attractively rather than blubbering nonsense onto her pink shoulder. She just hangs on with all her strength, as though she were a baby and not a grown girl of eight.

"You must be exhausted," her grandmother says. Natia can't quite tell how she winds up in the open carriage, her bundle on her feet and her grandmother's arm around her. "Let's get you home and a bath and some clean clothes on you. That will feel better."

Natia thinks that she hasn't eaten since a bowl of pottage last night at one of the posting stops, but it's hard to ask. Still, she might. "Do you think I might have some bread?" she asks. "I haven't eaten today, you see. If you don't mind."

Her grandmother's lips compress into a tight line, and Natia wonders where she got that scar. It looks like the ones the seminarians had from dueling. Surely grandmothers don't duel. "Idiot priest. Doesn't know anything about taking care of a child. Of course you can have some bread. We'll have lunch as soon as we get home. Stupid lout. He was ready to just leave you at the posting house, if some kind woman hadn't paid to send a message boy."

The carriage stops and for a moment Natia is confused. It's a florist shop, the windows full of tulips. Her grandmother doesn't go in, but leads to the door next to it, a neat black door with a brass knocker. "I have the top three floors," she says. "The first floors all along the street are shops, with town houses above. Come up and have some lunch, Natalie."

Natia stops at the top of the stairs. The drawing room is pretty and quiet, dark blue curtains framing the big windows. She stands there holding her bundle. Her grandmother speaks Polish. She can talk and have someone understand her. "Am I a bastard?" she says. It was not what she meant to say.

Her grandmother tosses her bonnet on the nearest chair. Her hair is honey colored, streaked with gray. "No," she says. "I know that Francis loved your mother." She gently takes the bundle out of Natia's hands and puts it on the table, helps her take her coat off as though she were very small.

"They weren't really married," Natia says. It's best to get the worst out of the way first. "My mother was no better than she should be and my father . . ."

"Was an impetuous young cavalry officer." Her grandmother sits down on the blue brocade sofa so that their eyes are on a level.

"I'm like them," Natia says. "I'm bad. I'm too pretty and it worries people, and I have bad blood."

Her grandmother raises a hand as though to caress her, stops as though she thinks better of it. There's a long scar across her palm too, and the back of her hand is covered in tiny white scars like snowflakes. "If so, you get it from me," she says. "I don't know what they told you about me. Probably not that I'm a courtesan and a scandal and a sometime actress."

"You have scars like a man," Natia says.

"I do," she says. "And I've fought like a man from one end of this bloodsoaked continent to the other. I'm not much of a guardian for a little girl."

"My mother had men who paid her," Natia says quickly. "I can turn my back. Please don't send me away! I don't know where I'll go!"

Her mouth twitches as though some thought was arrested, but her voice is level. "I'm not going to send you away. Not now, not ever. You are my grandchild, my son's daughter, and I will never send you away. And I will do my very best not to get you into trouble. I promise that." She does reach out now and brush back Natia's hair from her brow. "As for being too pretty, well, I hope that you won't need to get by on your looks. But it's good to have them just in case. I'm not poor, and I hope you won't have to use them."

"To be a courtesan?"

"Or a spy," she says lightly. "Now I will ring for Cécile, and we'll have some lunch. It will all look better when you've had something to eat. I only hope that you won't hate me when you know me better."

Natia stands up very solemnly and came closer, looking into her face. Crows feet around blue eyes, graying hair and the scar.

She traces it with one finger tentatively. "Where did you get that?"

"Eylau," she says.

"And that?" She lifts her grandmother's hand and turns it over. The cut across her palm must have bit to the bone.

"Waterloo. I was wearing heavy gloves, so it didn't take my fingers off."

Natia nods quietly. "I won't hate you," she says.

"Good," says her grandmother.

That night, she sleeps for the first time in a room by herself, a pretty little room with toile drapes and a big warm bed. In the morning they are going to order clothes, but tonight she sleeps in one of her grandmother's chemises. It's much too big, but it's soft and clean, white lawn with no lace or ribbons, just sleek thin fabric.

There are no men in the house. It's just her grandmother in her room and the housekeeper upstairs. If there were supposed to be men they aren't here. And Natia has her own room. She doesn't have to turn her back.

She sinks down into the big feather pillows.

Whatever happens next, tonight she is warm.

BRUNNHILDE IN THE FIRE
1901 AD

A nd at last the dawning twentieth century, a century that can
solve all problems through science. It has no need for magic.
Does it?

There are things men do, and women who let them do
it. She's gotten that far from whispers, from things girls
confide one to another in bedrooms where their mothers don't
come, whispered among the pillows of a featherbed while the
adults have dinner downstairs. She is not yet a debutante. She
does not sit at dinner. Not until next winter.

She is fifteen still, not sixteen until the high winter stars of
January shine cold on the ice, born under the sign of Capricorn
in the Year of Our Lord 1886. There is meaning to that, to
the stars that shone upon her birth, but her mother says such
superstitions are for the credulous, for Eastern European
immigrants who crowd the streets of Boston, dirty and speaking
foreign languages she thinks she should understand. If she just
listened a little longer, the words would be plain. But she never
listens more than a moment. Even the scullery maid who sweeps
the ashes is Irish. Her mother will not have filthy Poles in the
house.

There are things men want to do. It goes without saying that
women don't want to. Women want children and respectable
marriages. Women want love. Love is entirely different.

Love is born in music, over songs sung together at the piano, voices mingling like captive birds taking flight. She could imagine a voice to blend with hers, practicing in the music room on long afternoons, when her voice soars sweet and true. She has not got the coloratura range, but it's a light, pretty soprano. She could make her way on it if she had to, some part of her thinks. She'd never be a diva, but she'd eat.

Not that she will ever have to. Her father says she is safe. She will never lack for anything.

She should practice more, her mother says. Music is an accomplishment. She will bend her brain reading so much. She'd like to go to school. There is Radcliffe, but her father disapproves. It turns out suffragettes and anarchists, and she will be a respectable wife and mother. Her tutor has French and a little Latin, but it is enough. Latin comes easily. She suspects she already reads better than her tutor. It's not a matter of codebreaking, as her brother says, of taking apart words with suffixes and prefixes, memorizing declensions. She just reads it. Latin is living and breathing.

Once, when they were younger, leaning over the table with Frank, the tutor between them, she saw another table, another boy with light brown hair, his brows creased just so. "It is my father's tongue," he said. "You would think it would be easier."

Her hands are pale, smoothing out the scroll before him, words in Latin cursive flowing off the page. "It gets easier," she says, and what she feels is tenderness for him. He is a son to her, and the memory is tinged with love.

And then it is Frank, frowning at De Bello Gallico. "I don't know why you think this is so easy," he grouses.

"I think I've read it before," she says.

She knows better than to say anything else.

Once, when she was a child, she dreamed that an angel opened her mouth. An angel with a sword of fire stood beside her in a ruined chapel, and he touched her throat and she knew all the songs in the world, spoke every story she had ever known. But when she woke they faded away to scraps and tatters.

Perhaps if she went to school she would have less time to dream, less time to write fragments that never quite fit together in composition books, fairy tales and strange stories.

Once, Lono came over the sea in a boat of reeds and sunlight. Gulls followed his passage, and sharks swam beside him . . .

When Alexander was in Asia, he dreamed of a wheel of fire . . .

Blood pounded in her ears, drumming out the seconds, the flying wedge elongating, powder smoke blowing straight toward them, curved epee drawing clear, charging unhesitating into shadow . . .

Sometimes she thinks she is nothing but a vessel, an empty thing meant to hold stories. She will never be a story, have a story. Life is waiting, moving from one beautiful room to another, while her spirit soars.

Except that the body is real. Lying by herself in her room at night, windows open to catch the Cape Cod breeze, the ocean wind does not cool her. Her hands stray over her breasts, stroke the soft curve of her stomach. Ventre, some part of her says. That is what someone calls it when they kiss there.

The thought makes her draw sharp breath. The prickle of five o'clock shadow against her skin, warm lips kissing a path down her stomach . . .

She has never thought such an awful thing in her life! Who would do such a thing? And yet the rush of delight that follows after drowns out guilt. She is only thinking.

Composition books, and neat social script.

I am Undine in the pool
And Brunnhilde in the fire
Gyrecompass and prisoner
Of the wings that I inspire.

Her brother, Frank, hands it back to her seriously. "Brunnhilde was a Valkyrie doomed to live as a mortal woman," he says, "Not a safe thing."

And so she waits in her ring of fire, sleeping like Briar Rose on a bed of petals, looking out through white curtains at the world.

Once there was a princess sleeping forever in a chapel in a city of brass, where sand whispered over the mosaics on the floor, covering kings and queens among the lotus flowers . . .

The guns are silent all over the world, the mighty tumults of the last century ended. There will be no more wars, and knights only live in books. The modern world does not need them. King Arthur is beautifully illustrated on her bookshelf, Alexander tamed by Droysen. The modern world is tidy, classified, scientific, everything in its place like ornaments in her mother's étagère, curious relics of places and peoples one shouldn't think too hard about, Chinese porcelain and Egyptian boxes, a curious necklace of links of iron wrought into flowers.

I had one like that, some part of her whispers, looted when Berlin fell. It is a cold necklace of iron, a collar of steel, a cold irony that heats against the skin . . .

She dreams of flying, white wings beating far out to sea, soaring over waves and daring every storm. She wakes with tears on her face and cannot remember why.

"There will be no more wars," her father says. "The Powers

have reached entente. And nobody else matters." He leans back in his chair. "You children will inherit a peaceful world."

And yet she hears the whisper in the back of her mind, "Do you think the knights sleep in the hollow hills? That they have nothing better to do?"

ABOUT THE AUTHOR

Jo Graham lives in North Carolina with her partner, their daughter, and a spoiled Siamese cat. She has a degree in military history and worked in politics for fifteen years before becoming a full time writer. Her other books include the Numinous World series *Black Ships*, *Hand of Isis* and *Stealing Fire*, as well as the Stargate Atlantis novels *Death Game*, *Homecoming*, *The Lost*, and the upcoming *The Avengers*, *Secrets* and *The Inheritors*. Her next book in the Numinous World, *Fortune's Wheel*, will be published in the summer of 2012 by Gallery Books. She can be found online at http://jo-graham.livejournal.com/.

Wanda Lybarger, the cover artist, has been a graphic artist for forty years. She lives in Georgia.

Curious about other Crossroad Press books?
Stop by our site:
http://store.crossroadpress.com
We offer quality writing
in digital, audio, and print formats.

Enter the code FIRSTBOOK
to get 20% off your first order from our store!
Stop by today!